Sports Illustrated KIDS

GRAPHIC NOVELS

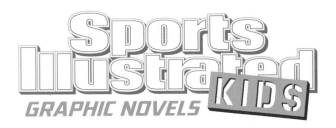

D1018028

STONE ARCH BOOKS
a capstone imprint

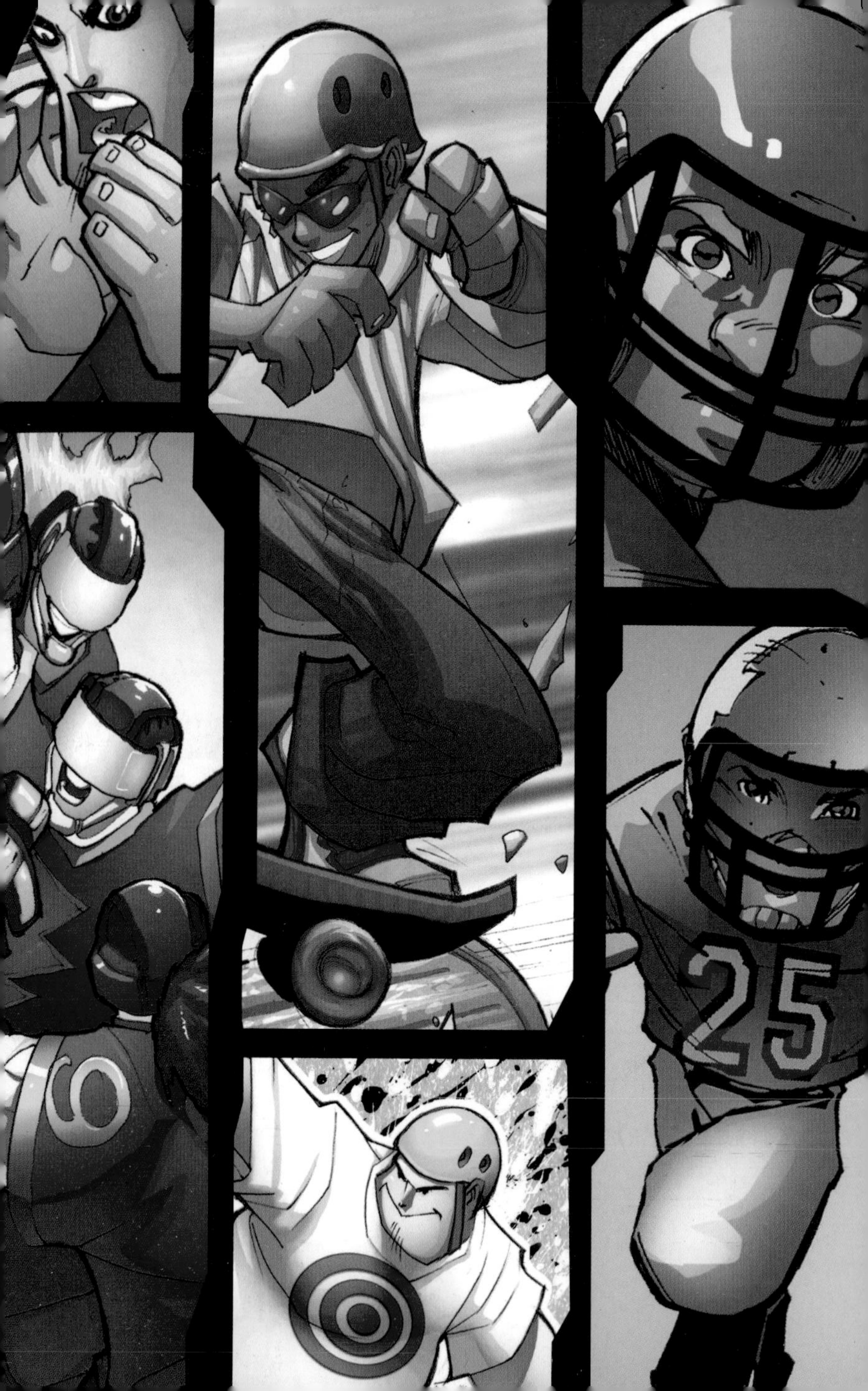
25

UP NEXT ›››

on Sports Illustrated KIDS

:02 SPORTS ZONE SPECIAL REPORT

:04 FEATURE PRESENTATION:

BATTLE for HOME PLATE

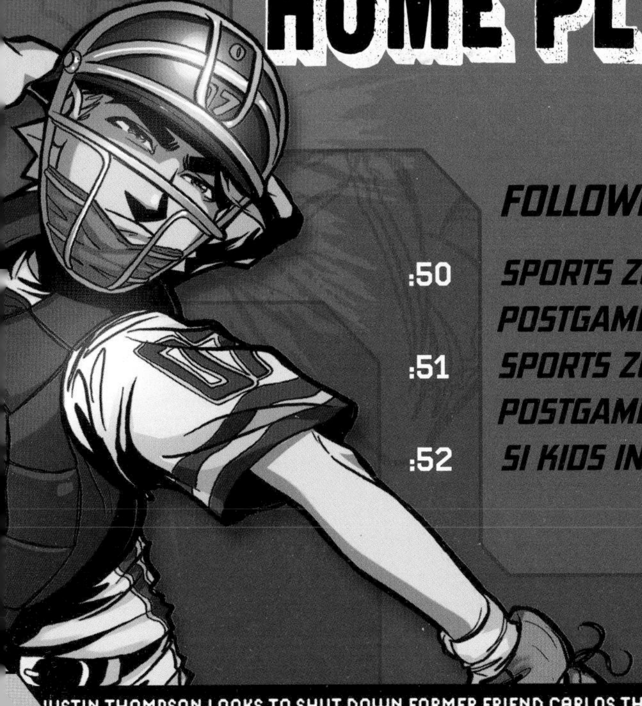

FOLLOWED BY:

:50 SPORTS ZONE POSTGAME RECAP

:51 SPORTS ZONE POSTGAME EXTRA

:52 SI KIDS INFO CENTER

USTIN THOMPSON LOOKS TO SHUT DOWN FORMER FRIEND CARLOS THIS SATUR

SIK TICKER

SPORTS ZONE

SPECIAL REPORT

SPARTANS CATCHER FACES FORMER FRIEND ON THE FIELD!

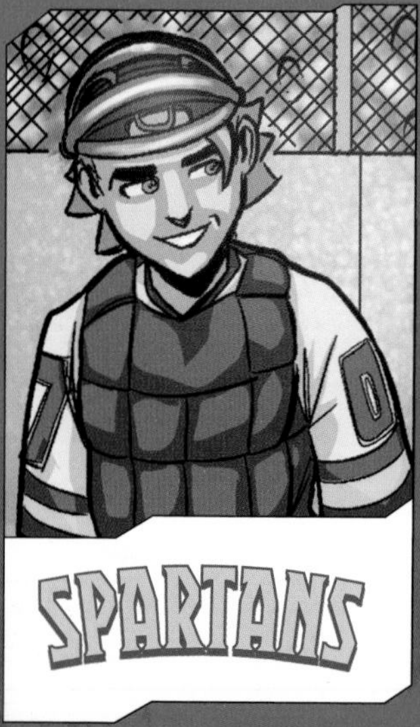
SPARTANS

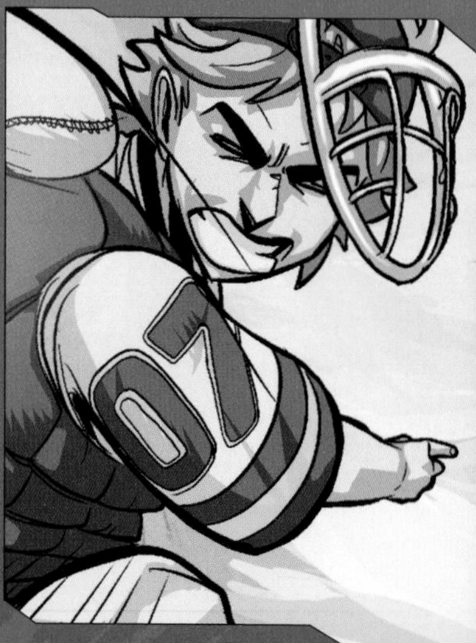

JUSTIN THOMPSON

STATS:
TEAM: SPARTANS
AGE: 14
NUMBER: 07
POSITION: CATCHER

BIO: Justin is a talented catcher and hitter who is also a loyal friend and teammate. He and Carlos Hernandez have been on the same team every year, and, as teammates, the two have made each other better players. But this year, they've found themselves on opposite sides of the field, which has thrown Justin off his game.

Sports Illustrated KIDS

UP NEXT: BATTLE FOR HOME PLATE

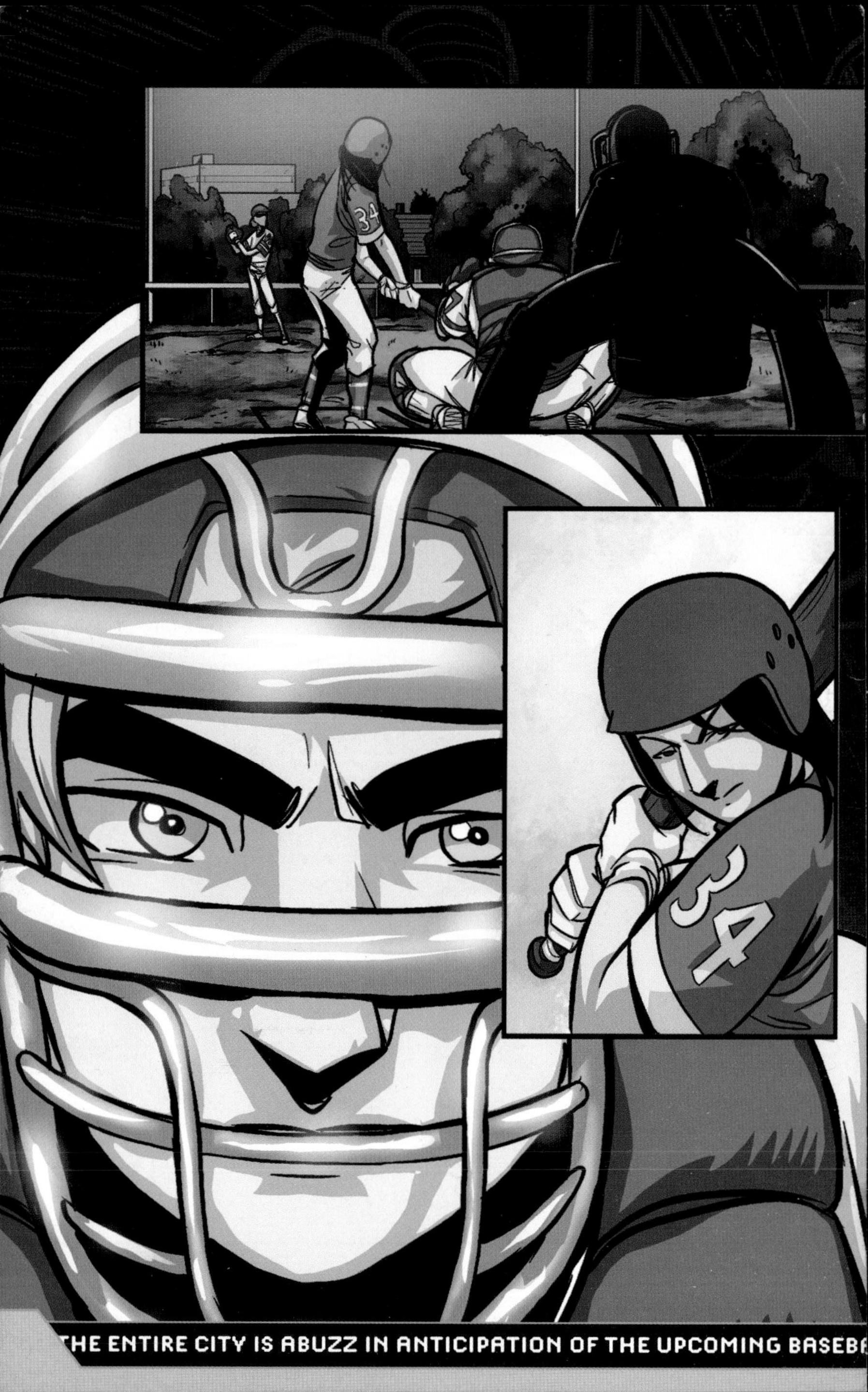

34
34
34
THE ENTIRE CITY IS ABUZZ IN ANTICIPATION OF THE UPCOMING BASEB

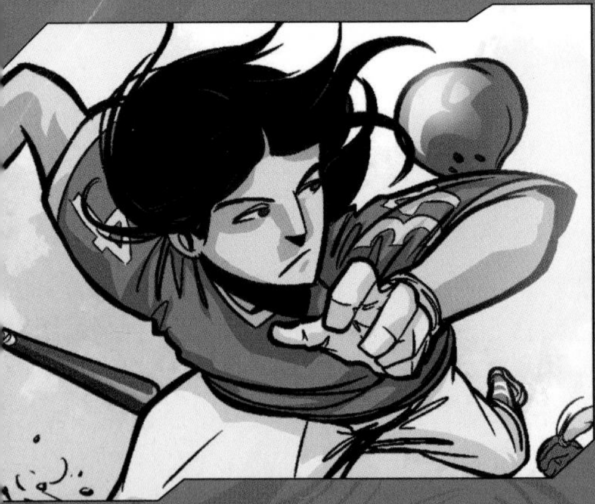

CARLOS HERNANDEZ

TEAM: WILDCATS
AGE: 14 **NUMBER:** 34
POSITION: PITCHER
BIO: Carlos throws hard and plays tough. He always wears a smile — until he and his best friend, Justin, end up playing on different teams.

BLZ vs BKS 3-1
TGR vs RDR 33-32
EAG vs BAN 14-7
SPA vs WLD 4-3
BAN vs RDR 21-15
RZR vs LIG 4-3
BLZ vs BKS 3-1
TGR vs RDR 33-32
EAG vs BAN

FREDDY LINCOLN

TEAM: WILDCATS **AGE:** 13 **POSITION:** CATCHER
BIO: Freddy is a top-notch catcher who helps the Wildcats pitchers perform at their very best.

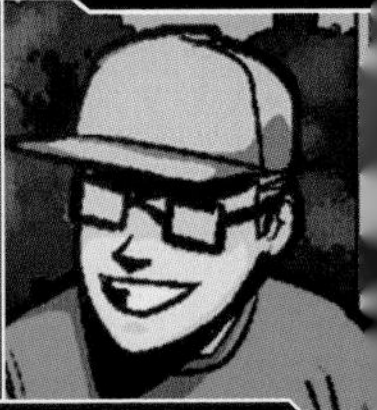

LINCOLN

RICARDO SPAN

TEAM: SPARTANS **AGE:** 46 **POSITION:** COACH
BIO: Coach Span is as intense as they come. He treats his players like adults, and expects 100 percent from them at all times.

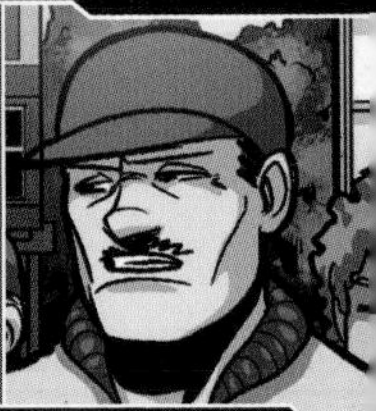

SPAN

ERIK DANIELS

TEAM: WILDCATS **AGE:** 33 **POSITION:** COACH
BIO: Coach Daniels is a friendly, soft-spoken man. He believes that the best way to coach is to keep his players upbeat and positive.

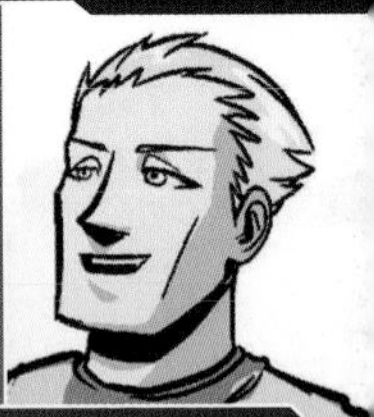

DANIELS

THE SPARTANS SAY THEY'RE READY FOR WHATEVER CARLOS THROWS AT THE SIK TICKER

Sports Illustrated KIDS

PRESENTS

BATTLE for HOME PLATE

A PRODUCTION OF

STONE ARCH BOOKS
a capstone imprint

written by Chris Kreie
illustrated by Jesus Aburto
colored by Fares Maese
Andres Esparza

designed and directed by Bob Lentz
edited by Sean Tulien
creative direction by Heather Kindseth
editorial direction by Michael Dahl

Sports Illustrated Kids *Battle for Home Plate* is published by Stone Arch Books,
1710 Roe Crest Drive, North Mankato, Minnesota 56003.
www.capstonepub.com

Summary: Justin and Carlos have played on the same baseball team since their T-ball days. But this season, the friends are forced to play on rival teams. Carlos makes new friends on the field, and Justin is left in the dust. When their teams face each other in the final game of the season, Justin and Carlos aren't even speaking. The game comes down to one run, and Carlos rounds third. What will happen when the former best friends collide at home plate?

Cataloging-in-Publication Data is available on the Library of Congress website.

ISBN: 978-1-4342-1913-8 (library binding)
ISBN: 978-1-4342-2290-9 (paperback)
ISBN: 978-1-4342-4939-5 (e-book)

Printed in the United States of America in North Mankato, Minnesota.
102016 010133R

FOR HOME PLATE BETWEEN THE WILDCATS AND THE SPARTAN SIK TICKER

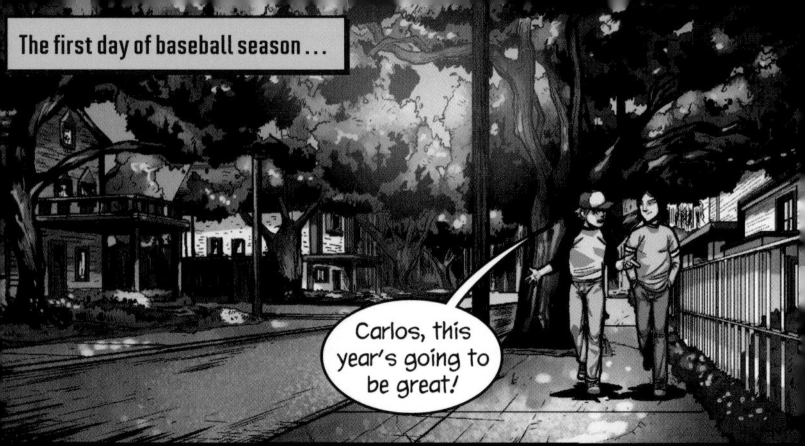
The first day of baseball season . . .
Carlos, this year's going to be great!

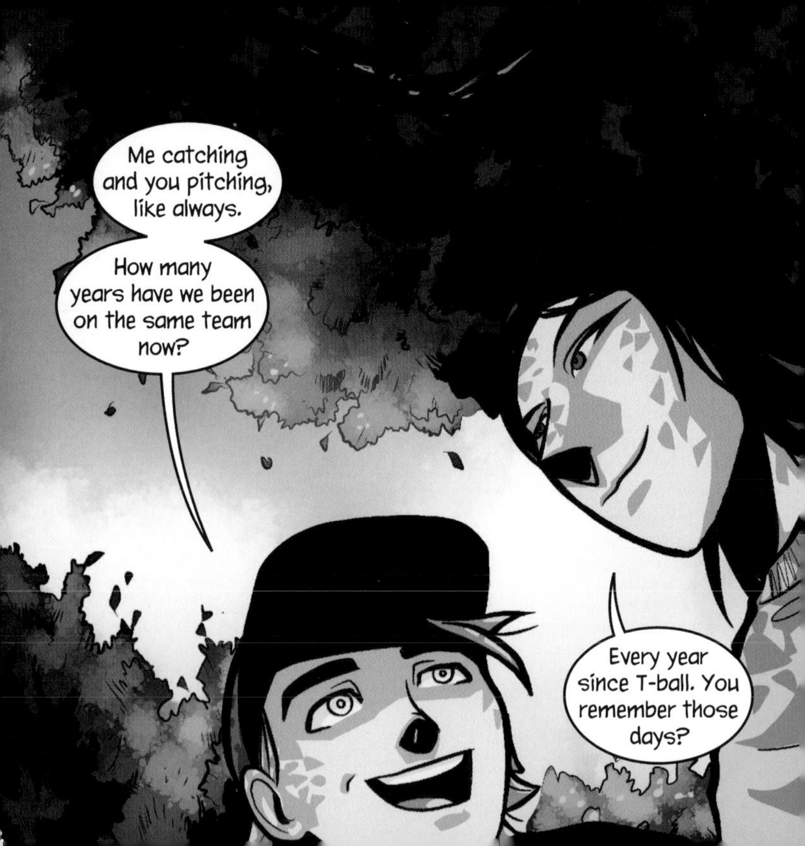
Me catching and you pitching, like always.
How many years have we been on the same team now?
Every year since T-ball. You remember those days?

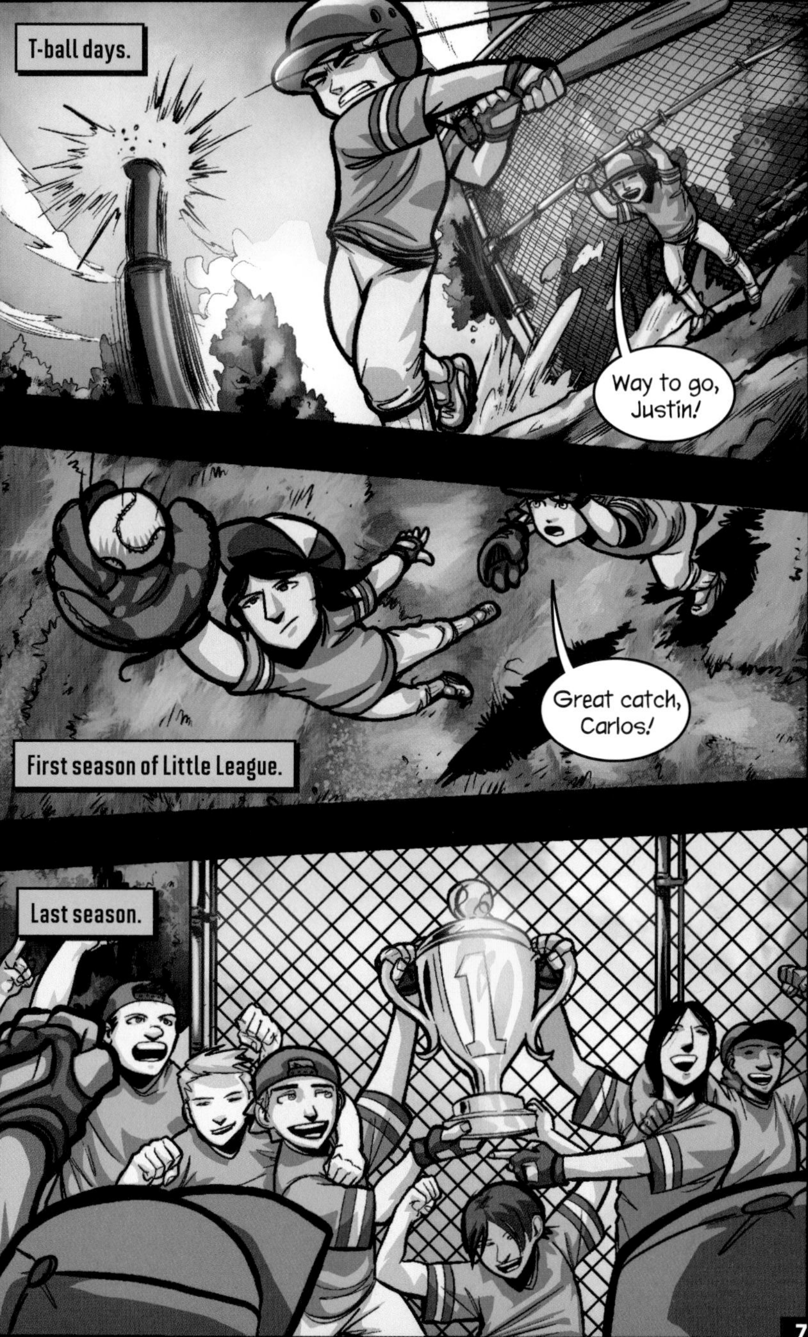
T-ball days.
Way to go, Justin!
Great catch, Carlos!
First season of Little League.
Last season.

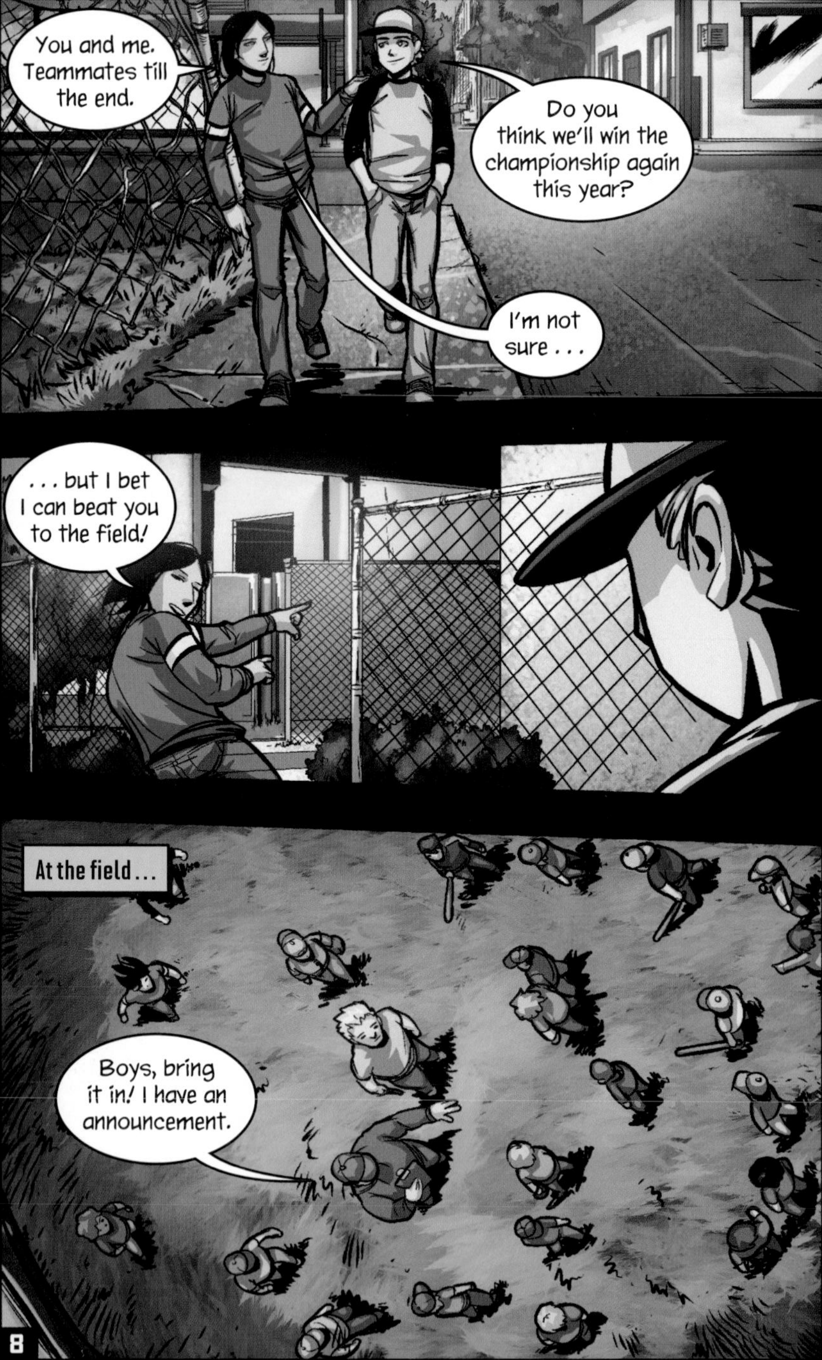
You and me. Teammates till the end.
Do you think we'll win the championship again this year?
I'm not sure . . .
. . . but I bet I can beat you to the field!
At the field . . .
Boys, bring it in! I have an announcement.

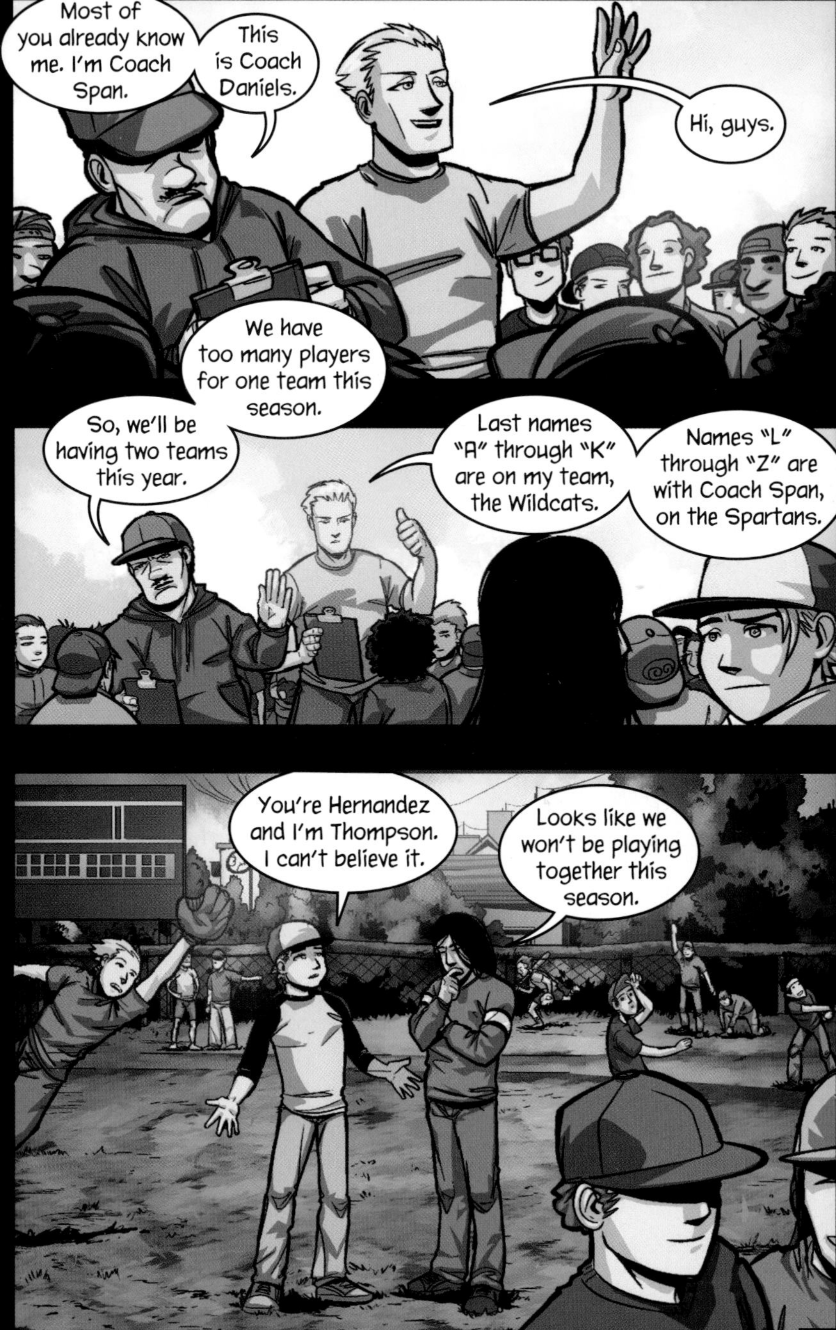

Most of you already know me. I'm Coach Span.
This is Coach Daniels.
Hi, guys.
We have too many players for one team this season.
So, we'll be having two teams this year.
Last names "A" through "K" are on my team, the Wildcats.
Names "L" through "Z" are with Coach Span, on the Spartans.
You're Hernandez and I'm Thompson. I can't believe it.
Looks like we won't be playing together this season.

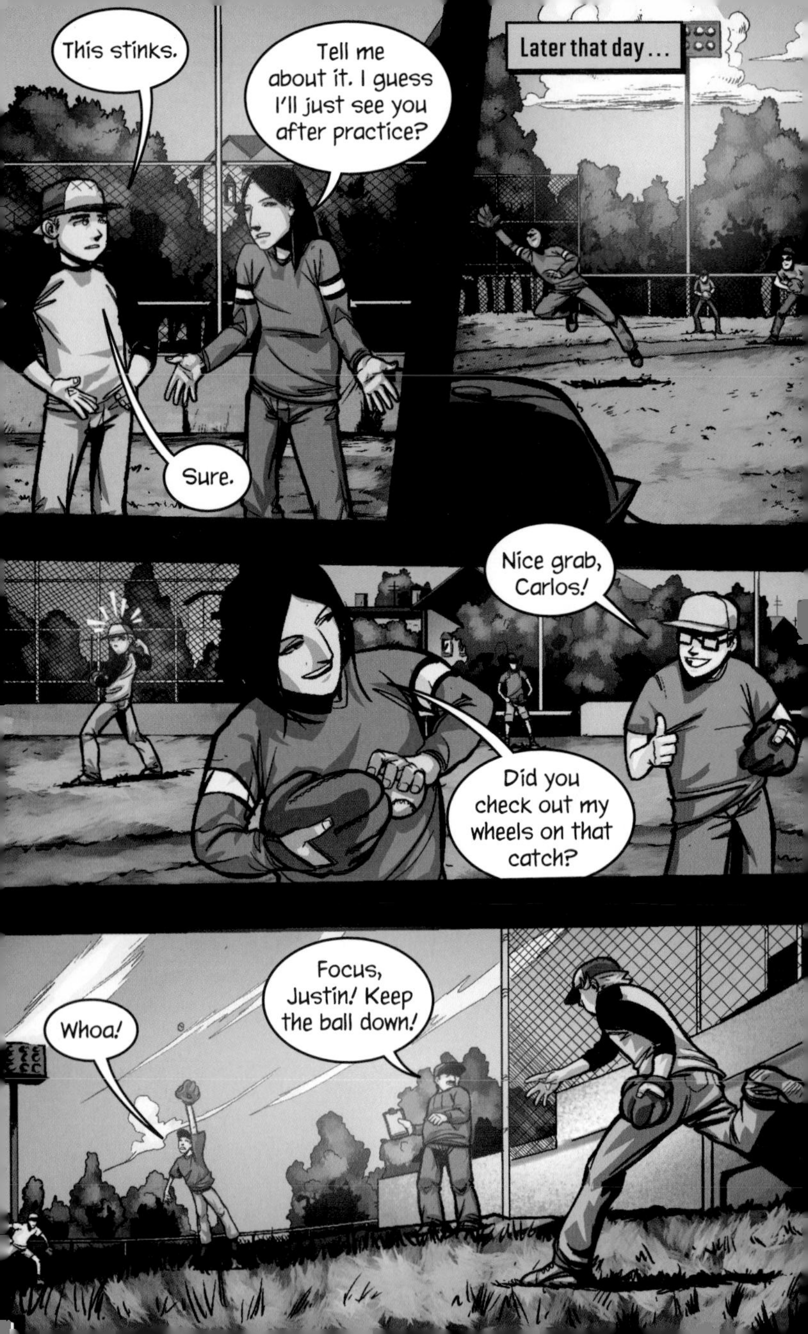
This stinks.
Tell me about it. I guess I'll just see you after practice?
Sure.
Later that day . . .
Nice grab, Carlos!
Did you check out my wheels on that catch?
Whoa!
Focus, Justin! Keep the ball down!

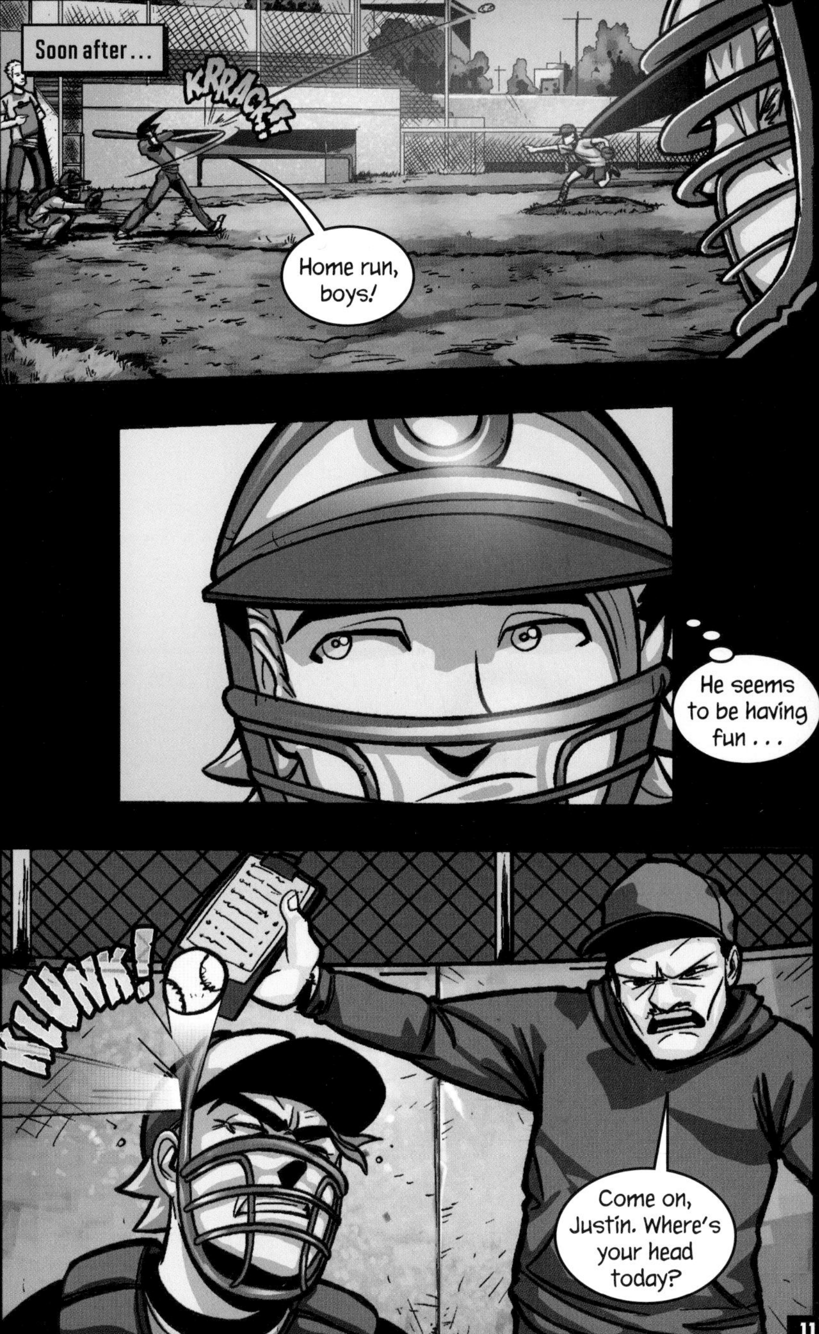
Soon after . . .
KRRACK!!
Home run, boys!
He seems to be having fun . . .
KLUNK!
Come on, Justin. Where's your head today?

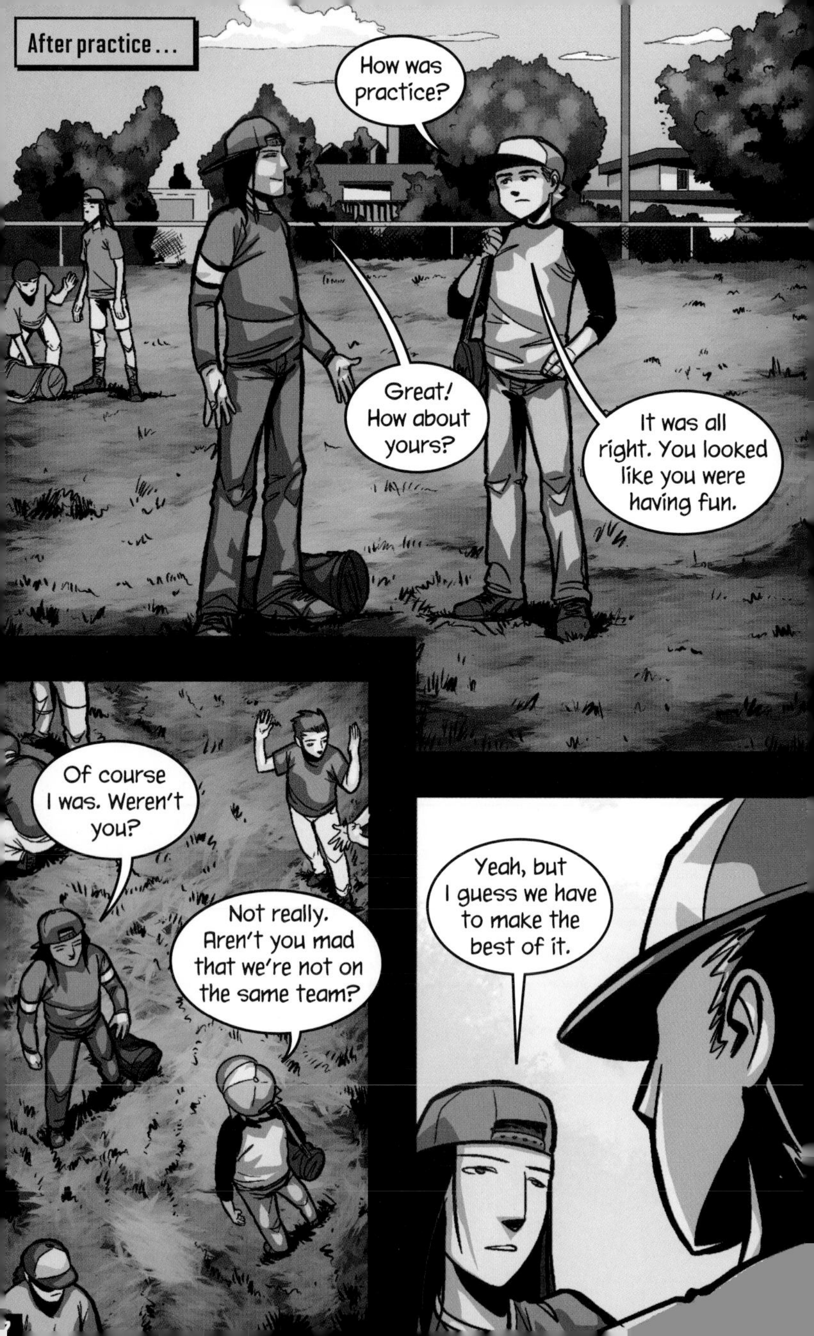
After practice . . .
How was practice?
Great! How about yours?
It was all right. You looked like you were having fun.
Of course I was. Weren't you?
Not really. Aren't you mad that we're not on the same team?
Yeah, but I guess we have to make the best of it.

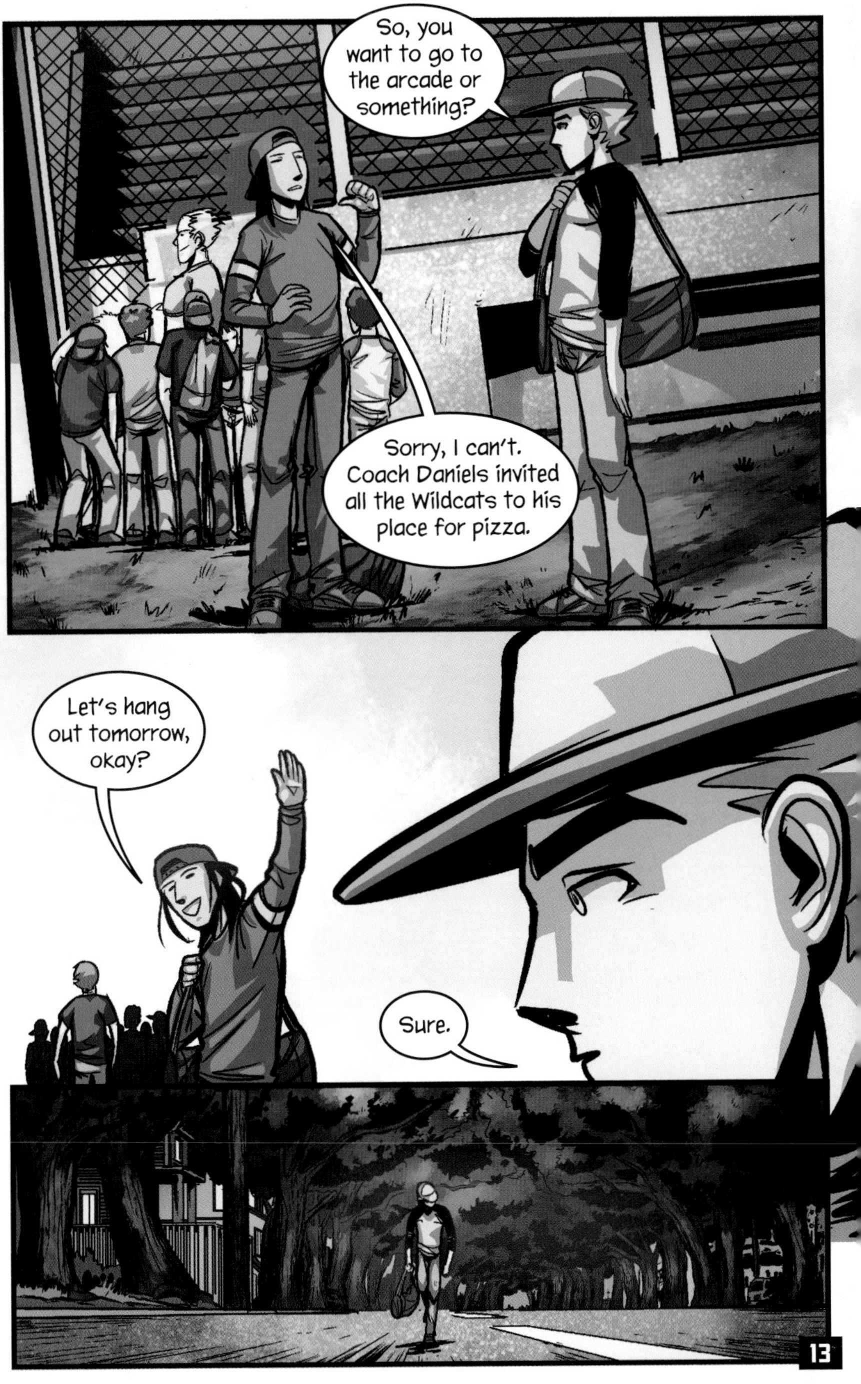

So, you want to go to the arcade or something?
Sorry, I can't. Coach Daniels invited all the Wildcats to his place for pizza.
Let's hang out tomorrow, okay?
Sure.

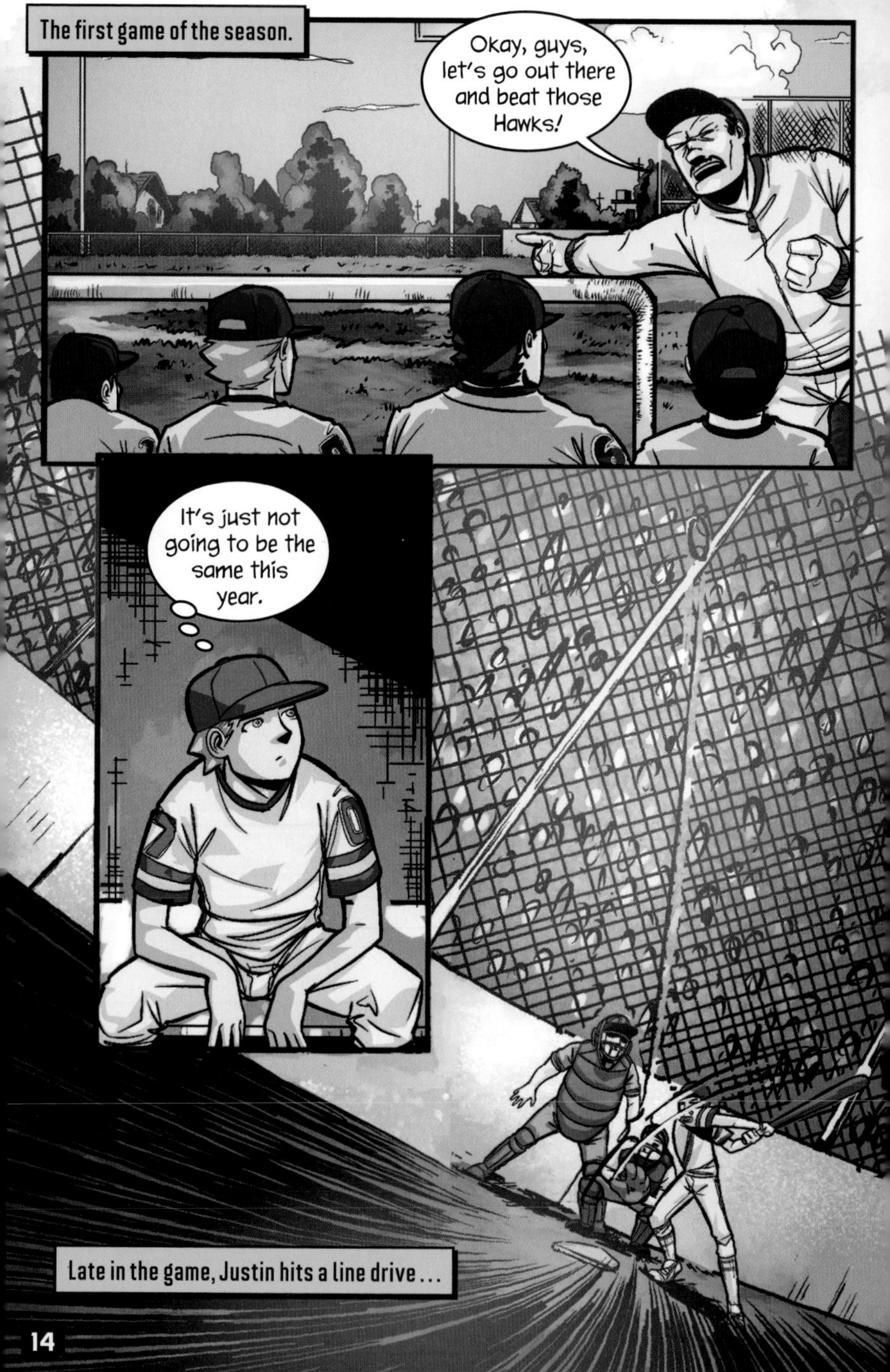

The first game of the season.
Okay, guys, let's go out there and beat those Hawks!
It's just not going to be the same this year.
Late in the game, Justin hits a line drive . . .

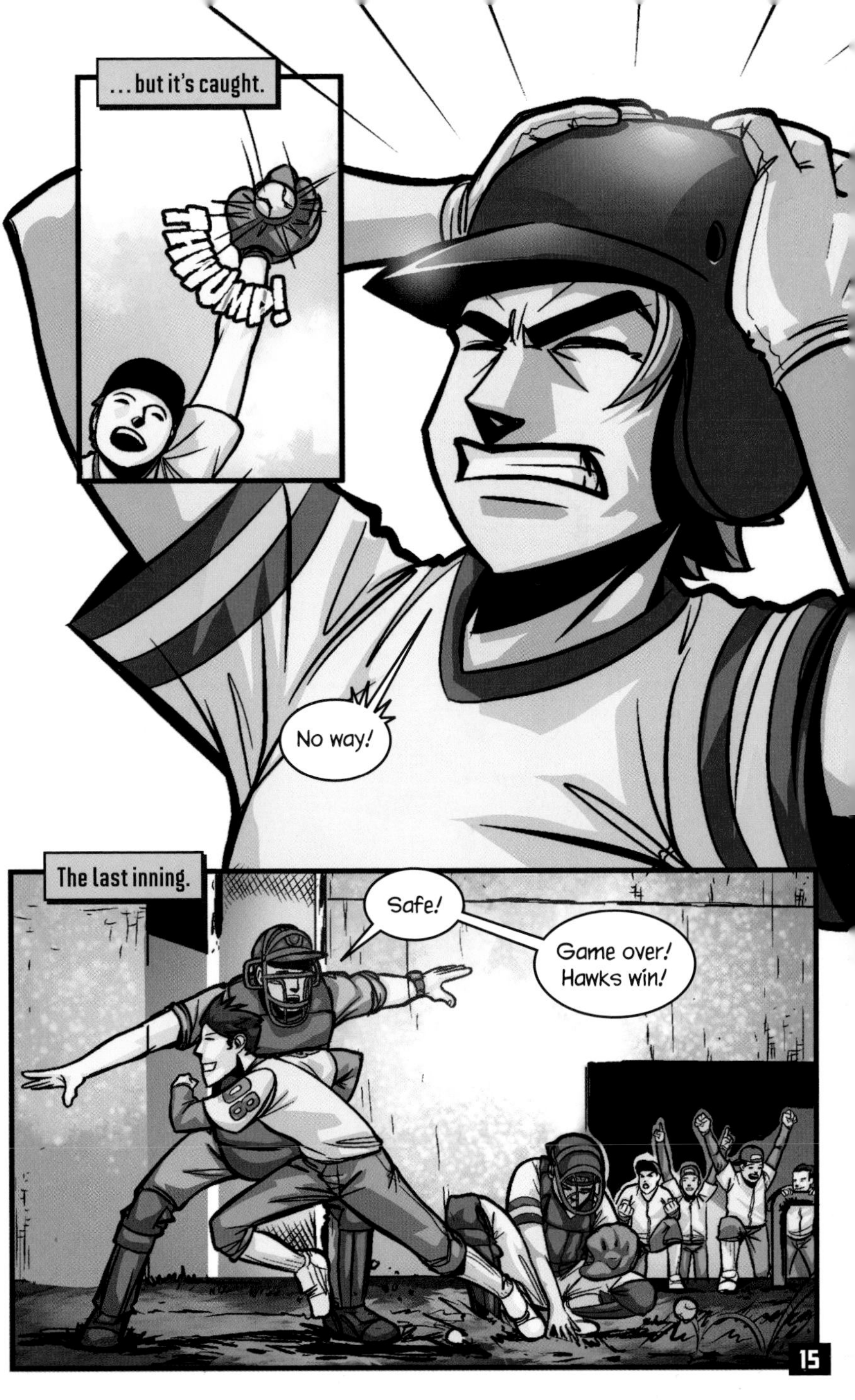

... but it's caught.
THWUMP!
No way!
The last inning.
Safe!
Game over! Hawks win!

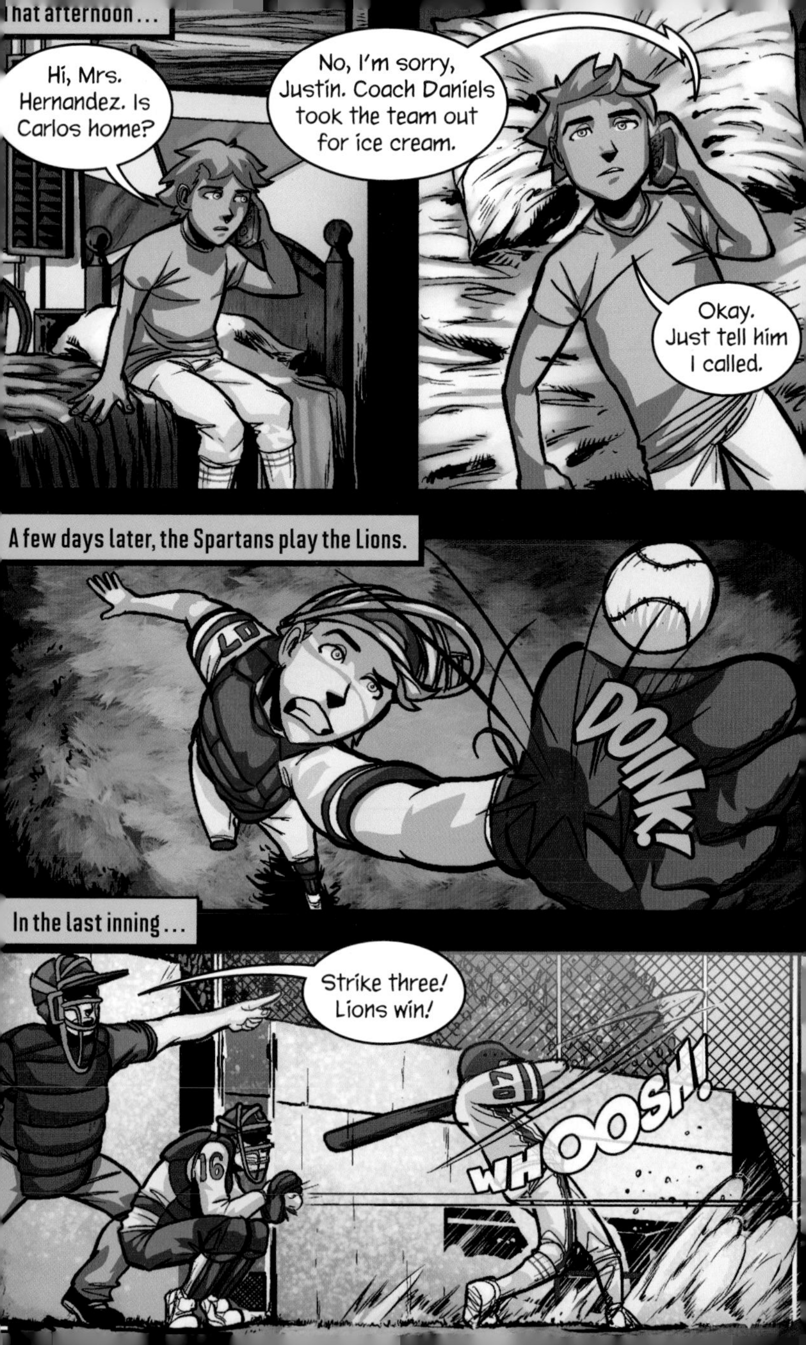
That afternoon . . .
Hi, Mrs. Hernandez. Is Carlos home?
No, I'm sorry, Justin. Coach Daniels took the team out for ice cream.
Okay. Just tell him I called.
A few days later, the Spartans play the Lions.
DOINK!
In the last inning . . .
Strike three! Lions win!
WHOOOSH!

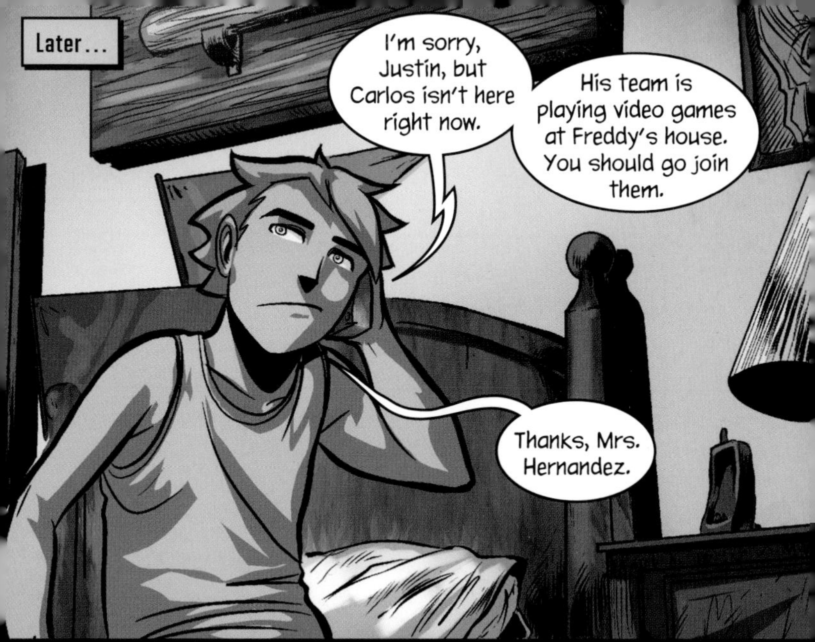
Later...
I'm sorry, Justin, but Carlos isn't here right now.
His team is playing video games at Freddy's house. You should go join them.
Thanks, Mrs. Hernandez.

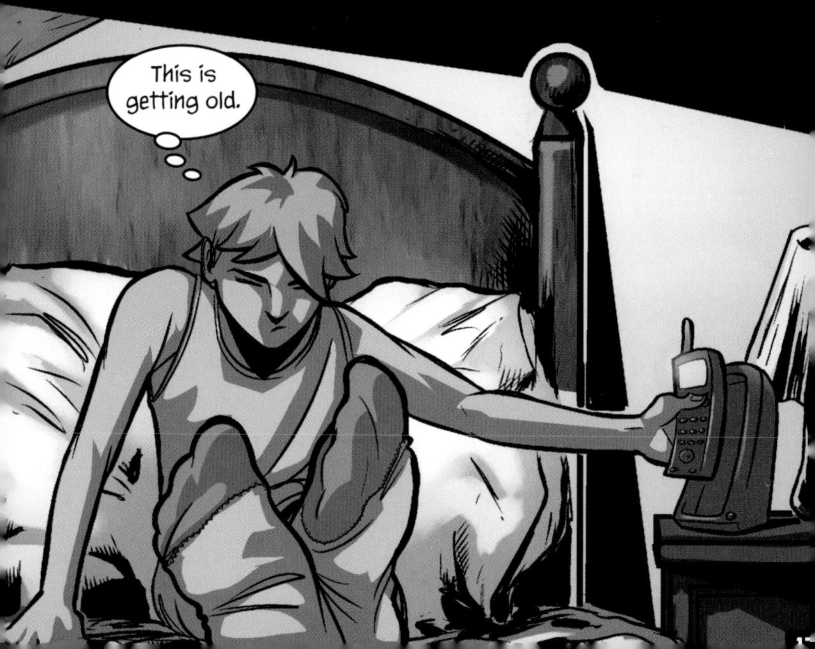
This is getting old.

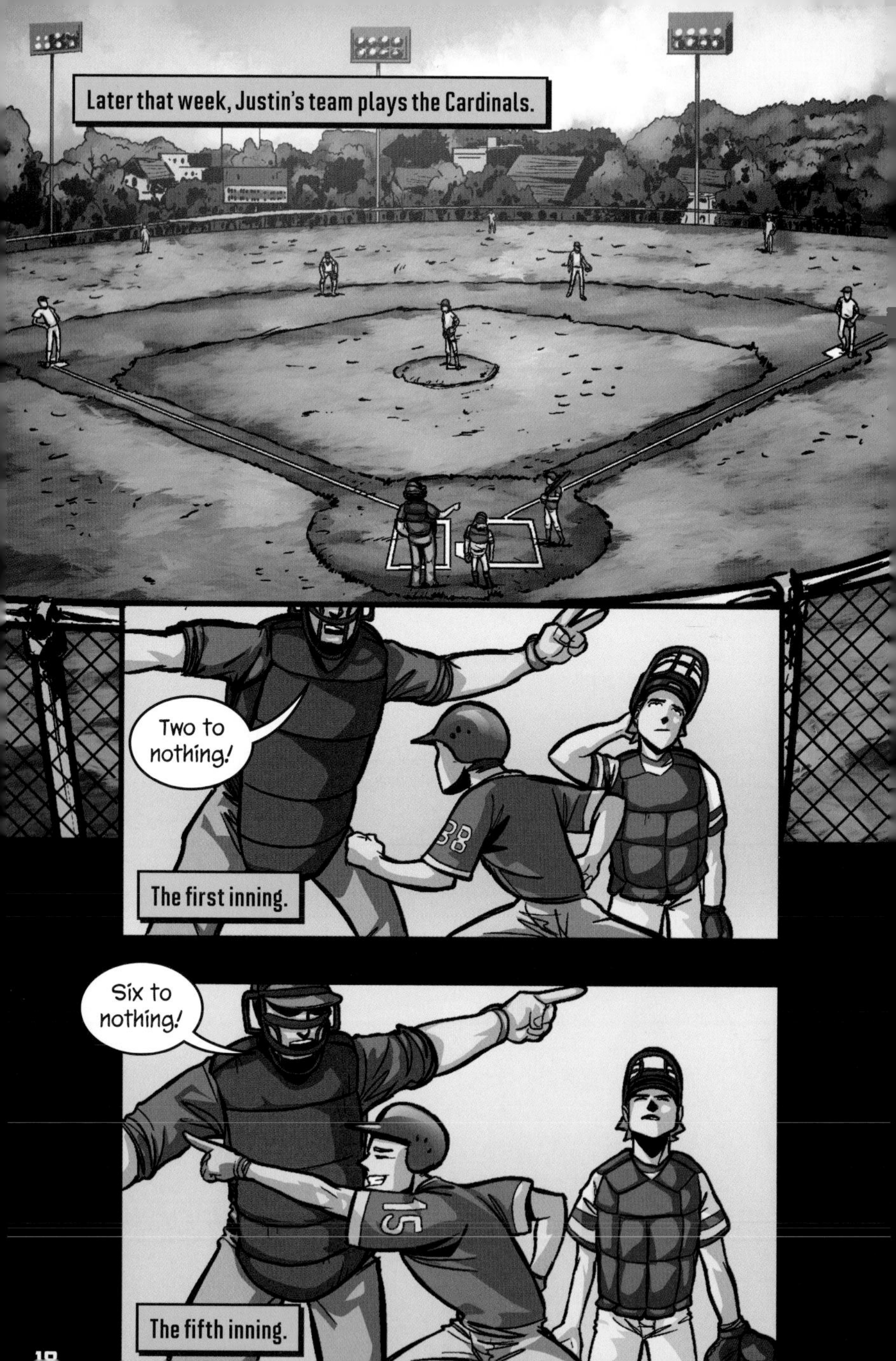
Later that week, Justin's team plays the Cardinals.
Two to nothing!
The first inning.
Six to nothing!
The fifth inning.

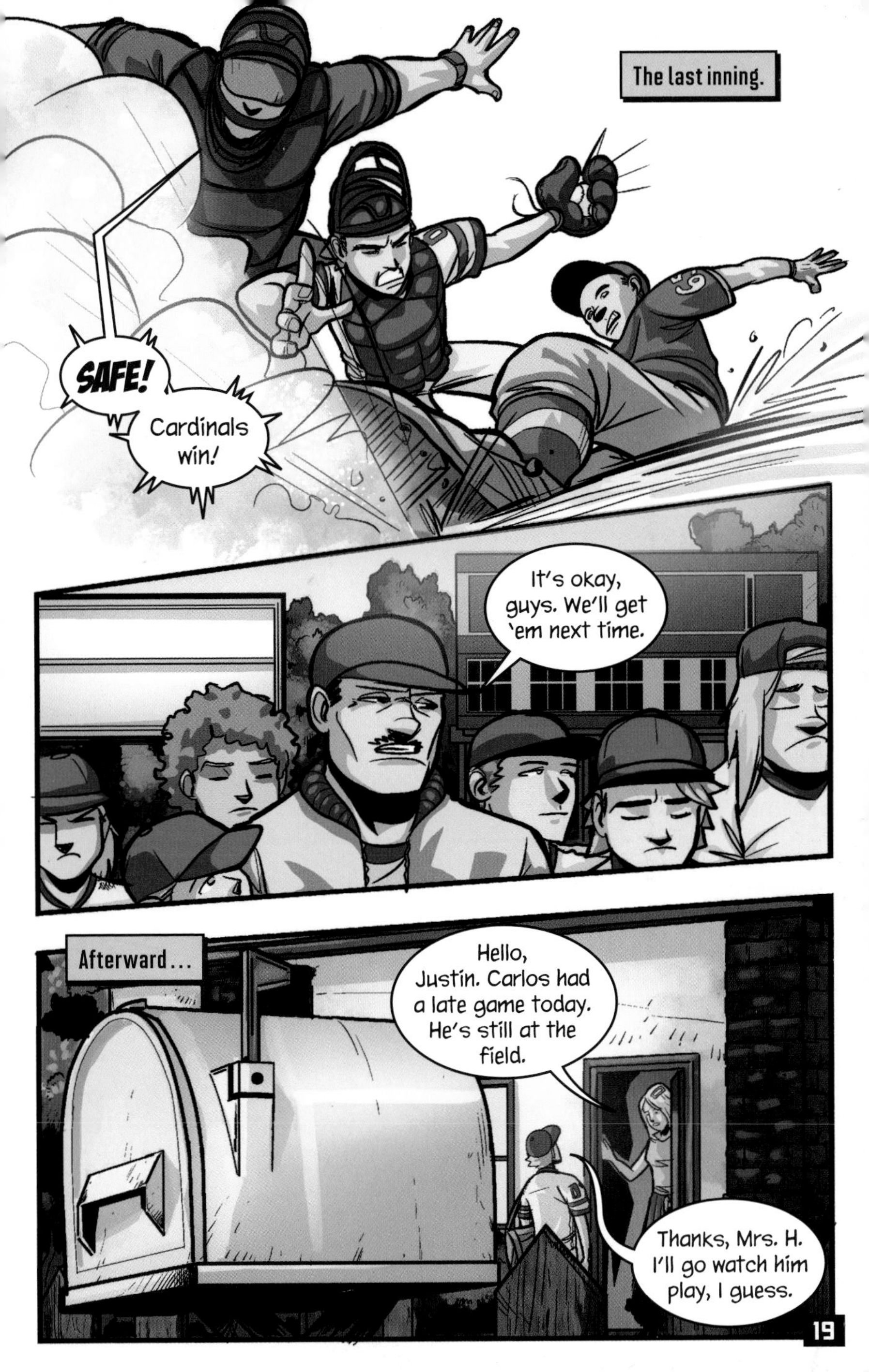

The last inning.
SAFE!
Cardinals win!
It's okay, guys. We'll get 'em next time.
Afterward...
Hello, Justin. Carlos had a late game today. He's still at the field.
Thanks, Mrs. H. I'll go watch him play, I guess.

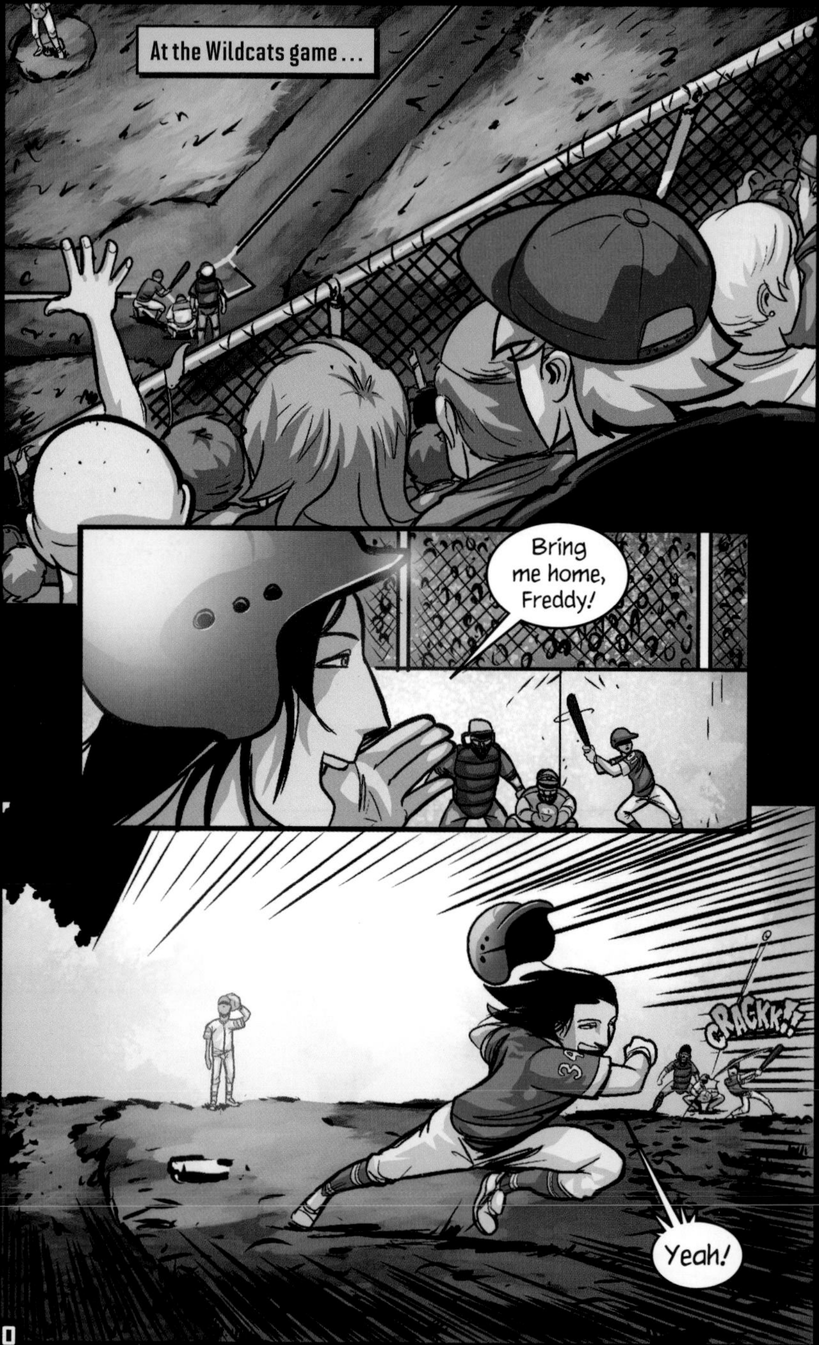

At the Wildcats game . . .
Bring me home, Freddy!
CRACKK!!
Yeah!

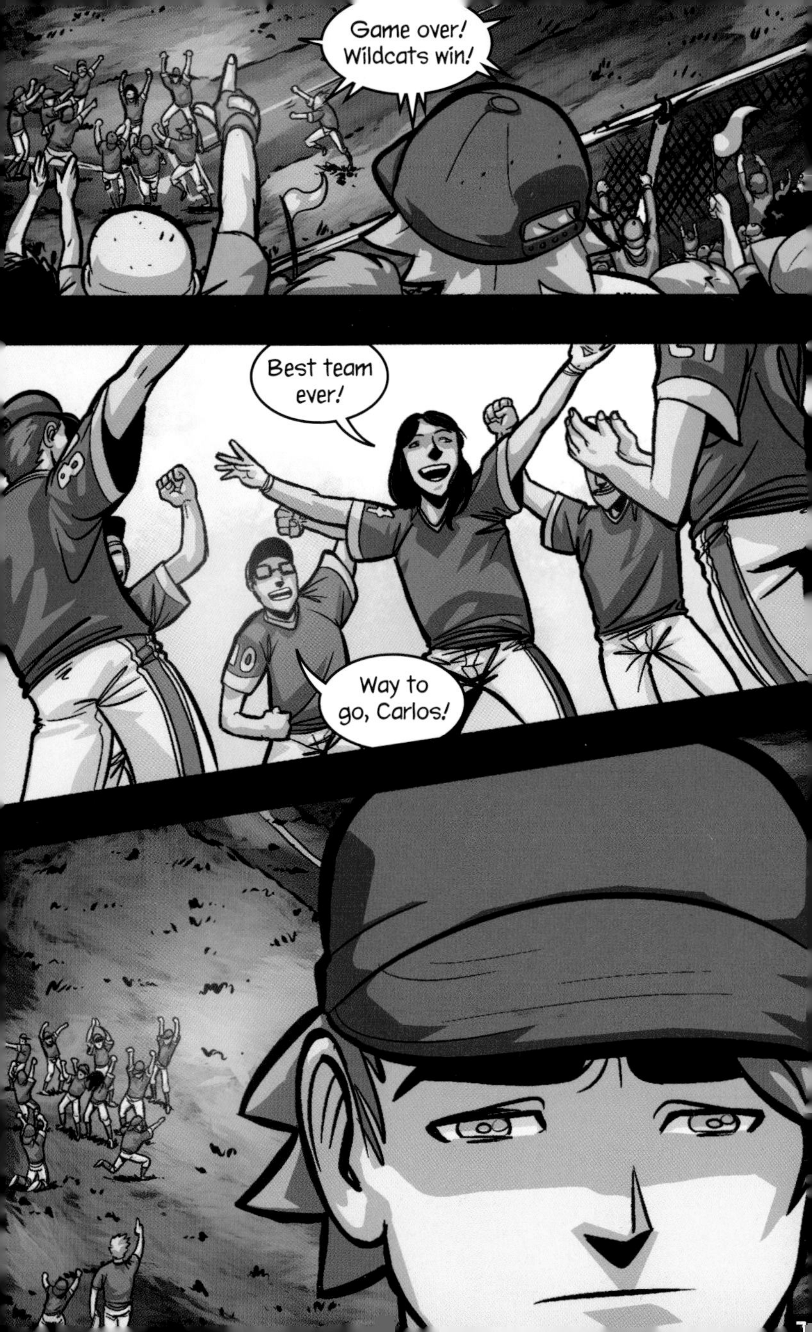
Game over! Wildcats win!
Best team ever!
Way to go, Carlos!

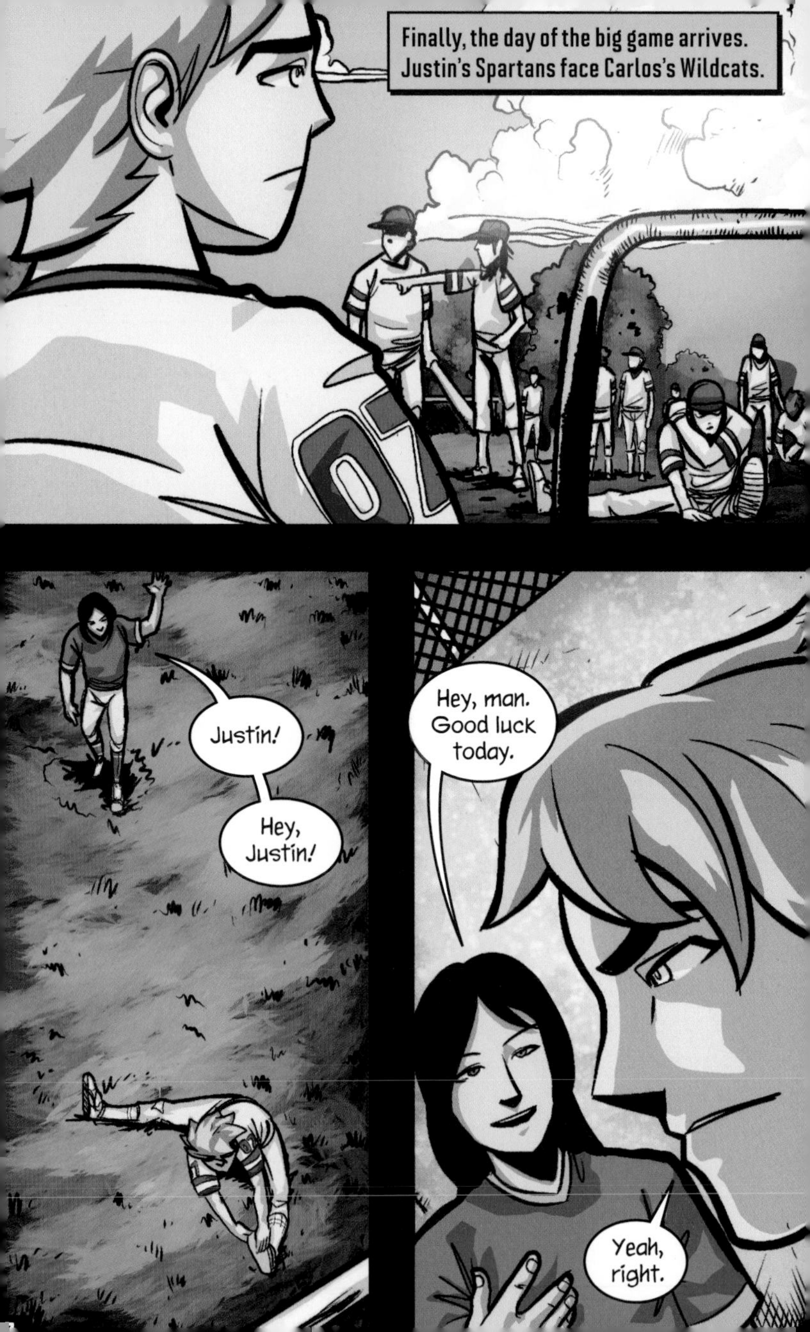
Finally, the day of the big game arrives. Justin's Spartans face Carlos's Wildcats.
Justin!
Hey, Justin!
Hey, man. Good luck today.
Yeah, right.

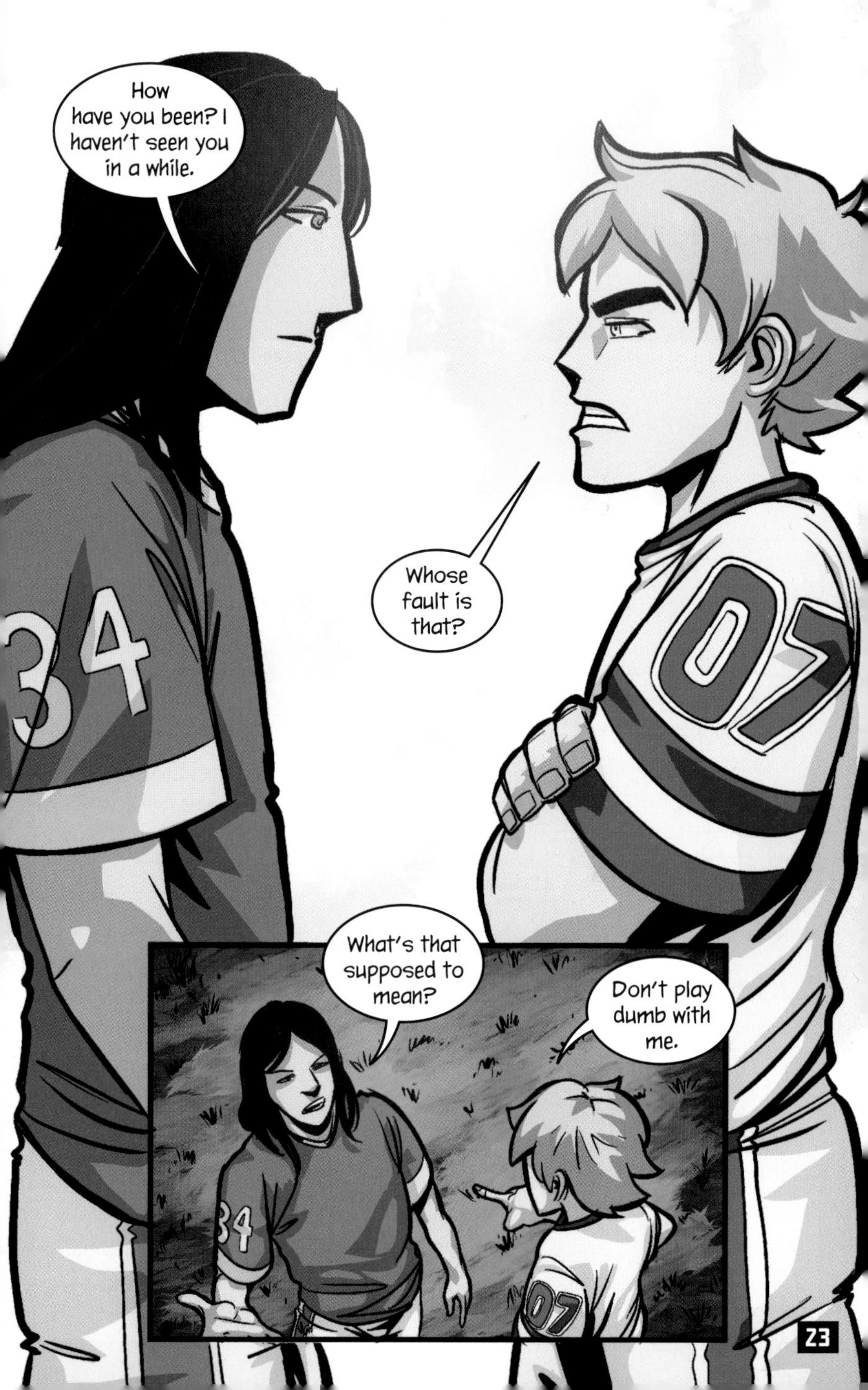
How have you been? I haven't seen you in a while.
Whose fault is that?
What's that supposed to mean?
Don't play dumb with me.

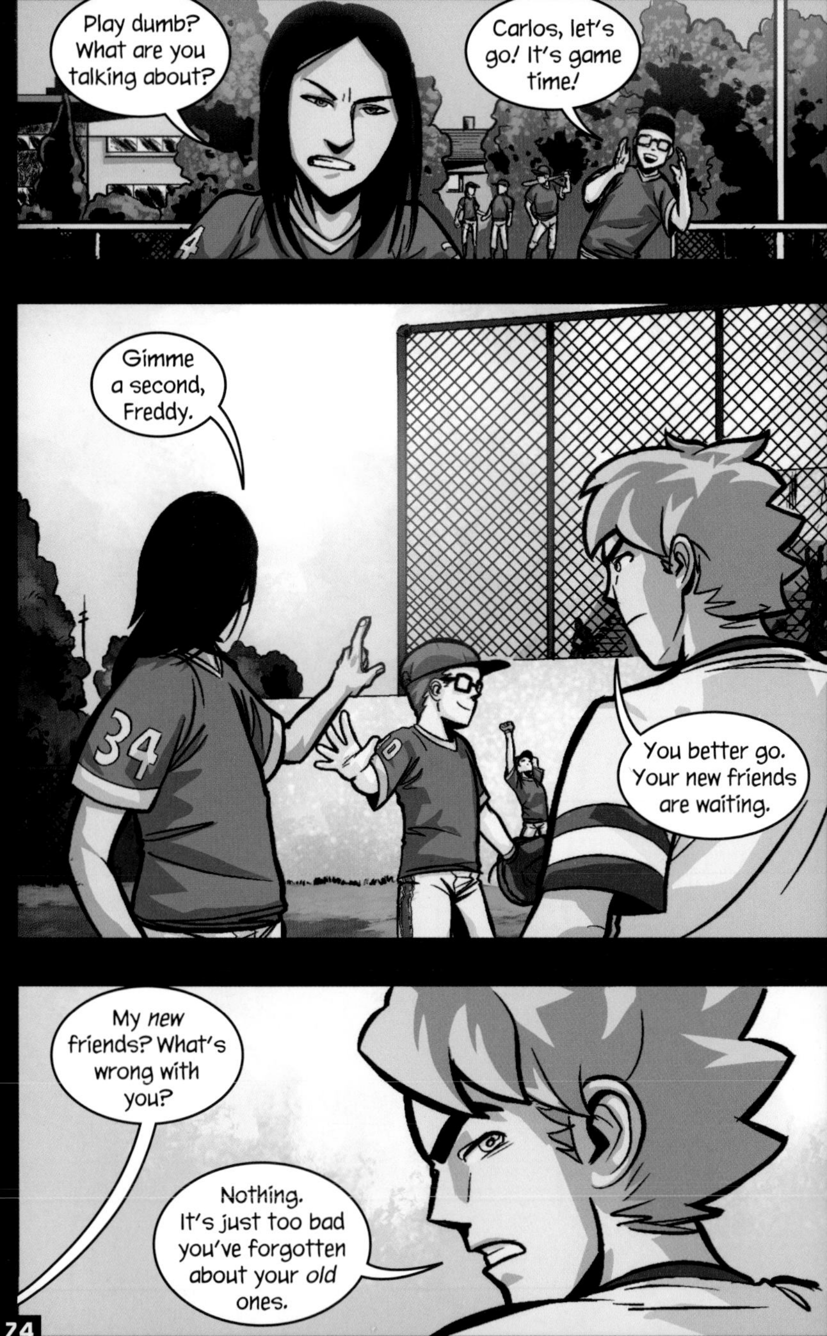
Play dumb? What are you talking about?
Carlos, let's go! It's game time!
Gimme a second, Freddy.
You better go. Your new friends are waiting.
My *new* friends? What's wrong with you?
Nothing. It's just too bad you've forgotten about your *old* ones.

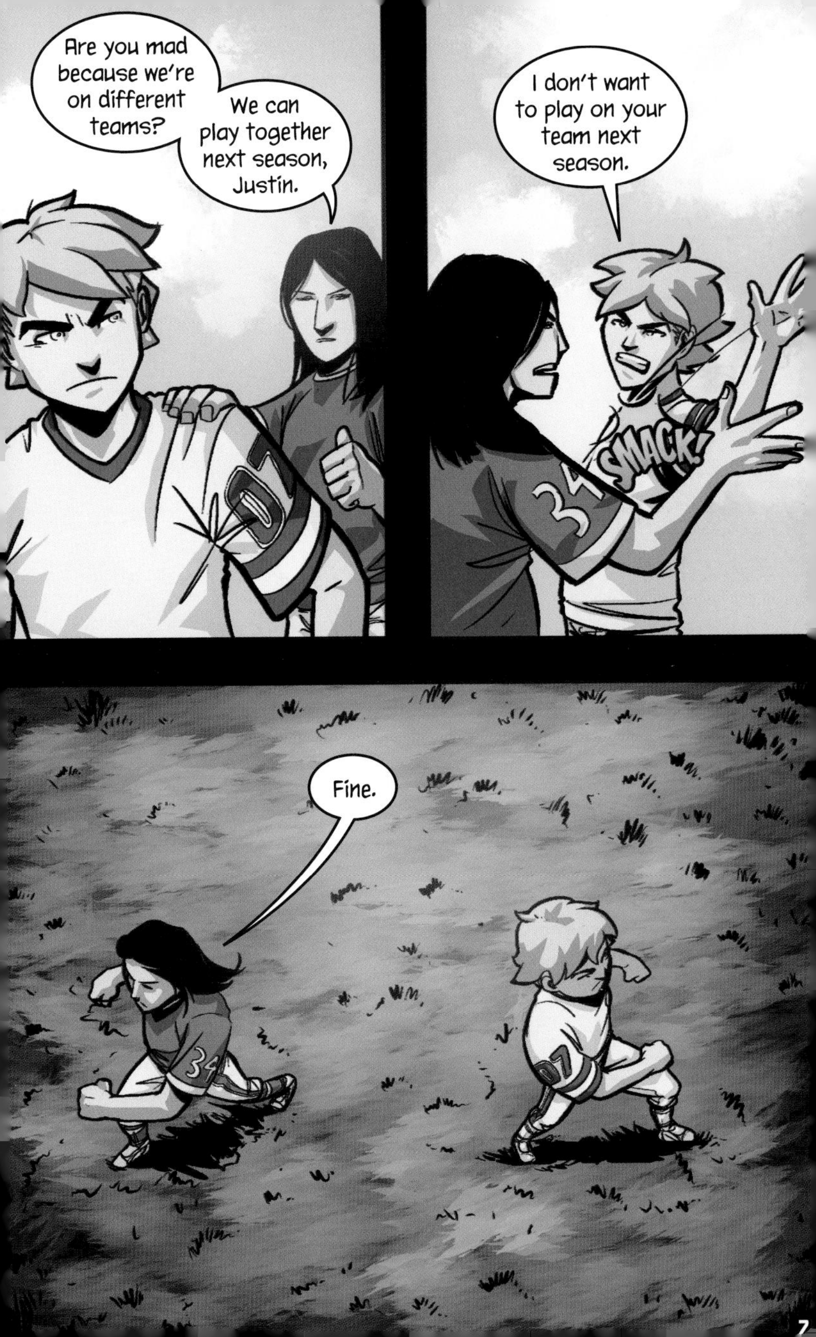
Are you mad because we're on different teams?
We can play together next season, Justin.
I don't want to play on your team next season.
SMACK!
Fine.

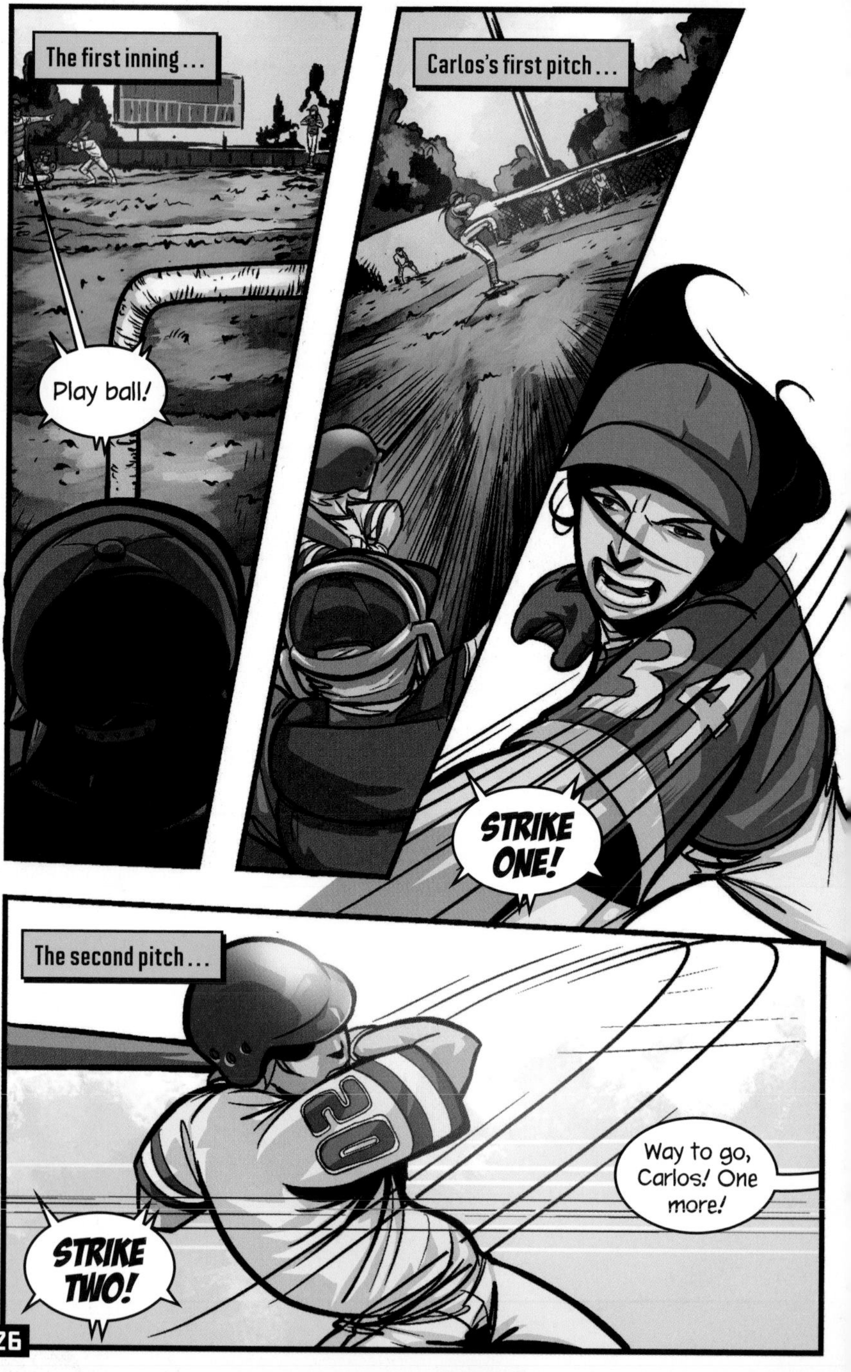
The first inning . . .
Play ball!
Carlos's first pitch . . .
STRIKE ONE!
The second pitch . . .
Way to go, Carlos! One more!
STRIKE TWO!

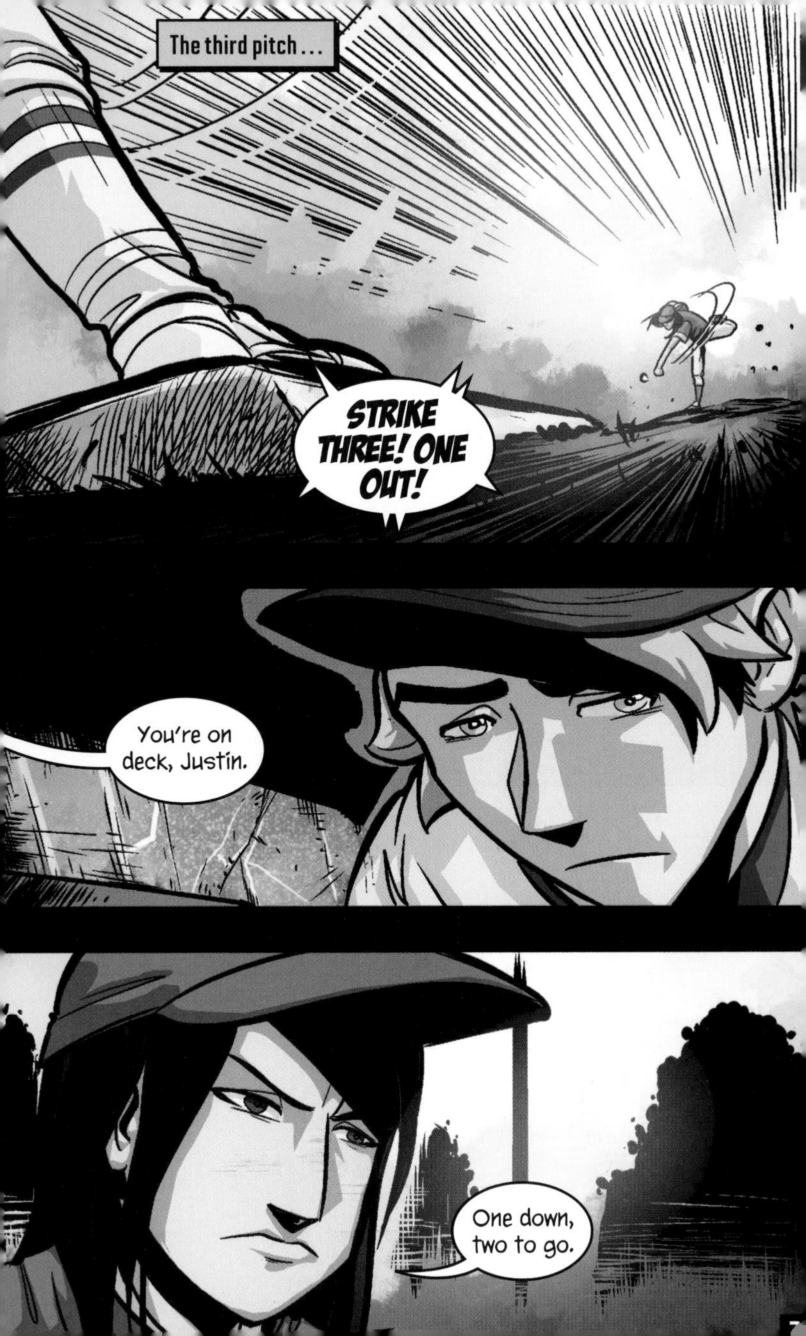
The third pitch . . .
STRIKE THREE! ONE OUT!
You're on deck, Justin.
One down, two to go.

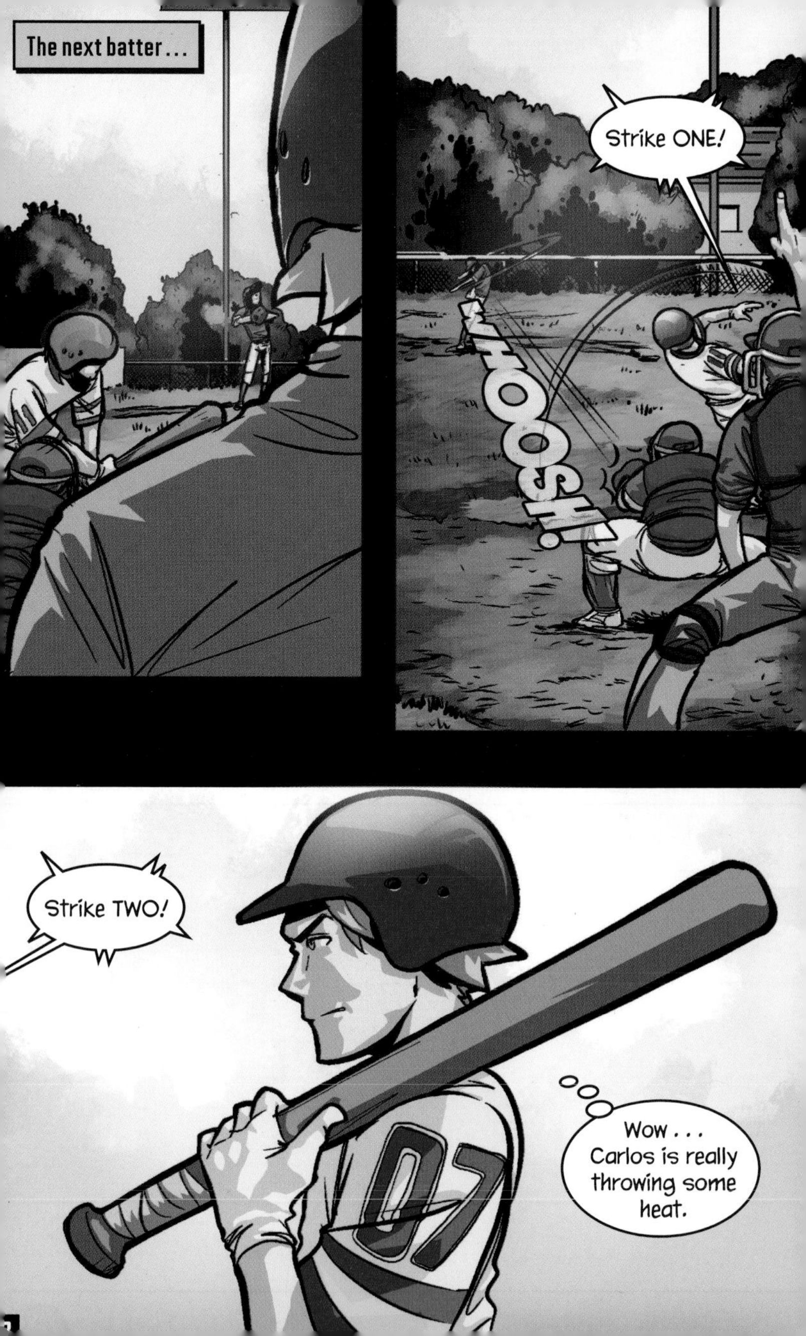
The next batter . . .
Strike ONE!
WHOOSH!
Strike TWO!
Wow . . . Carlos is really throwing some heat.

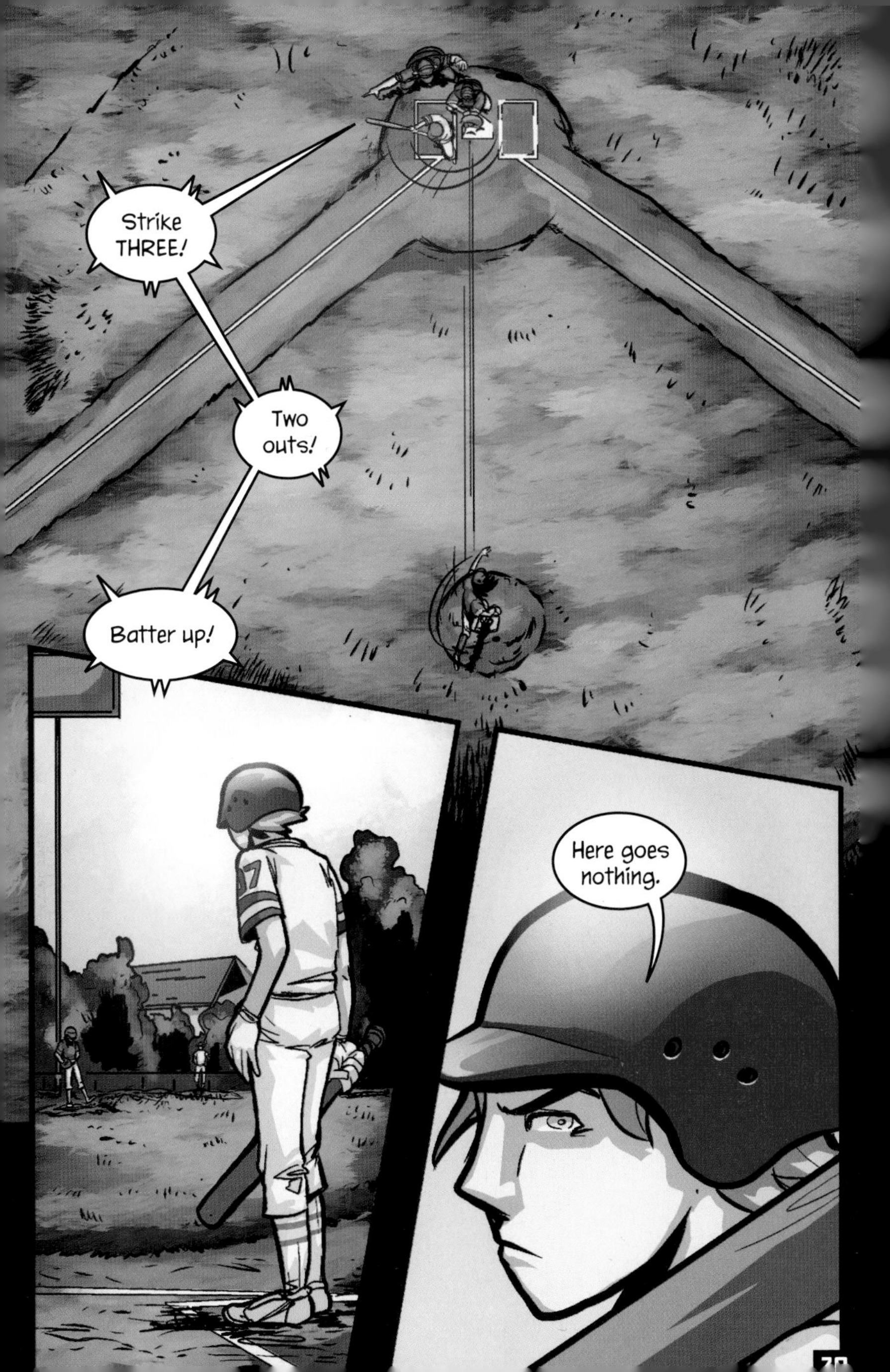
Strike THREE!
Two outs!
Batter up!
Here goes nothing.

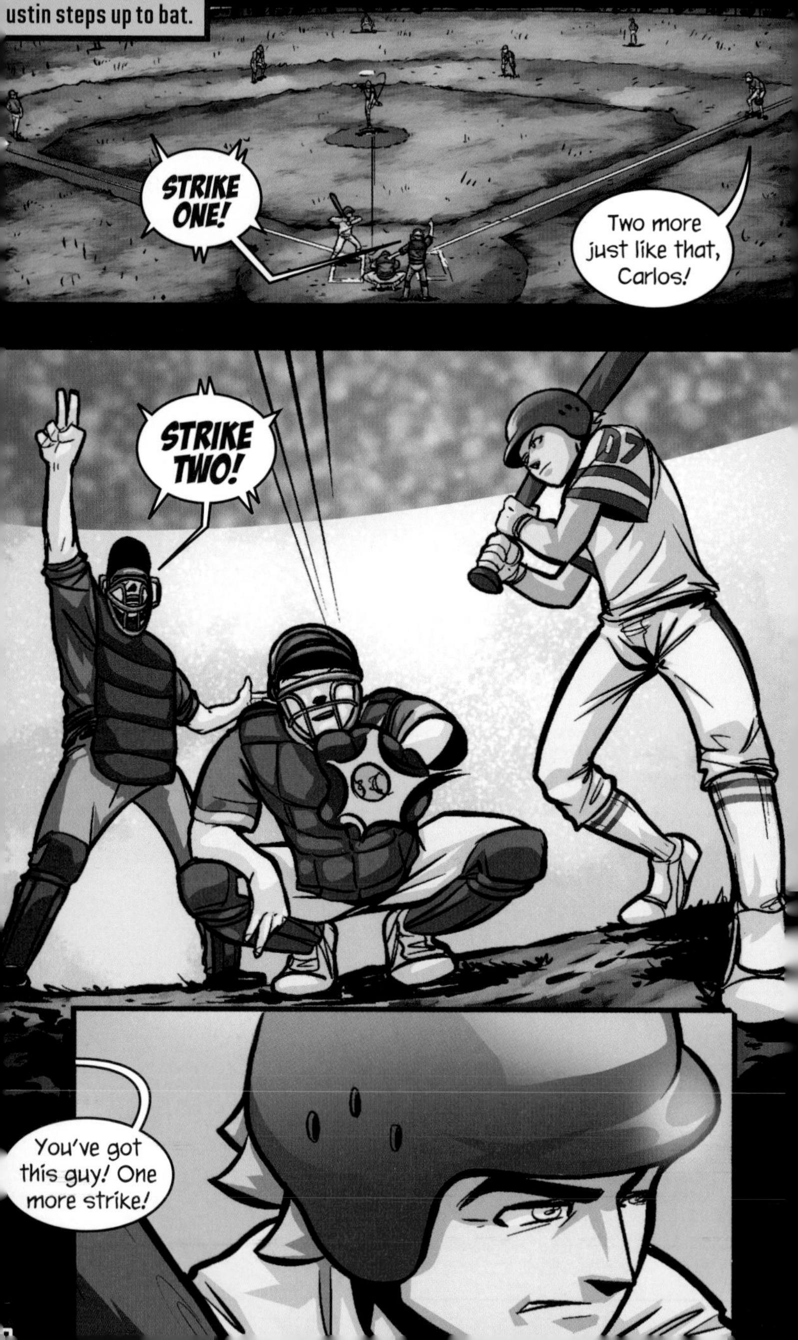
ustin steps up to bat.
STRIKE ONE!
Two more just like that, Carlos!
STRIKE TWO!
You've got this guy! One more strike!

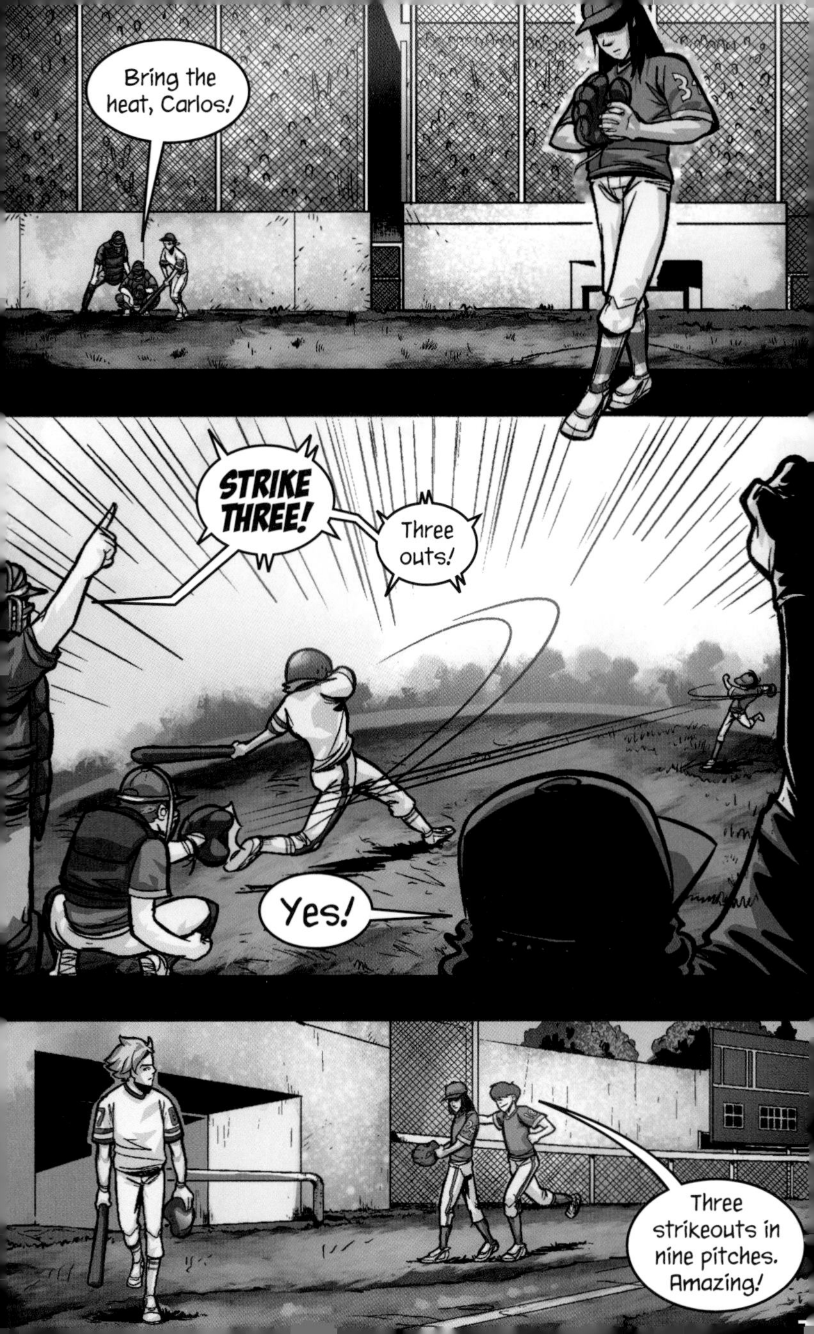
Bring the heat, Carlos!
STRIKE THREE!
Three outs!
Yes!
Three strikeouts in nine pitches. Amazing!

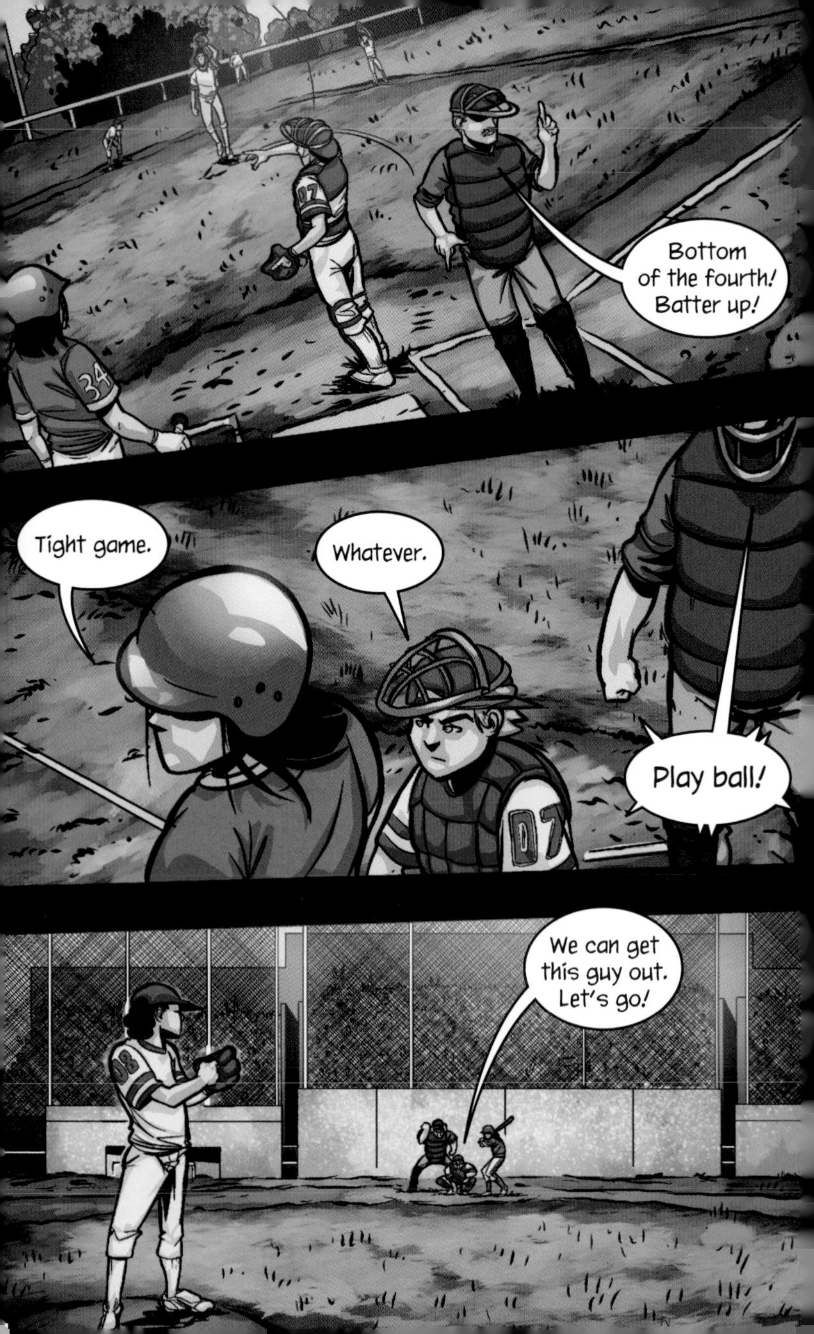

Bottom of the fourth! Batter up!
Tight game.
Whatever.
Play ball!
We can get this guy out. Let's go!

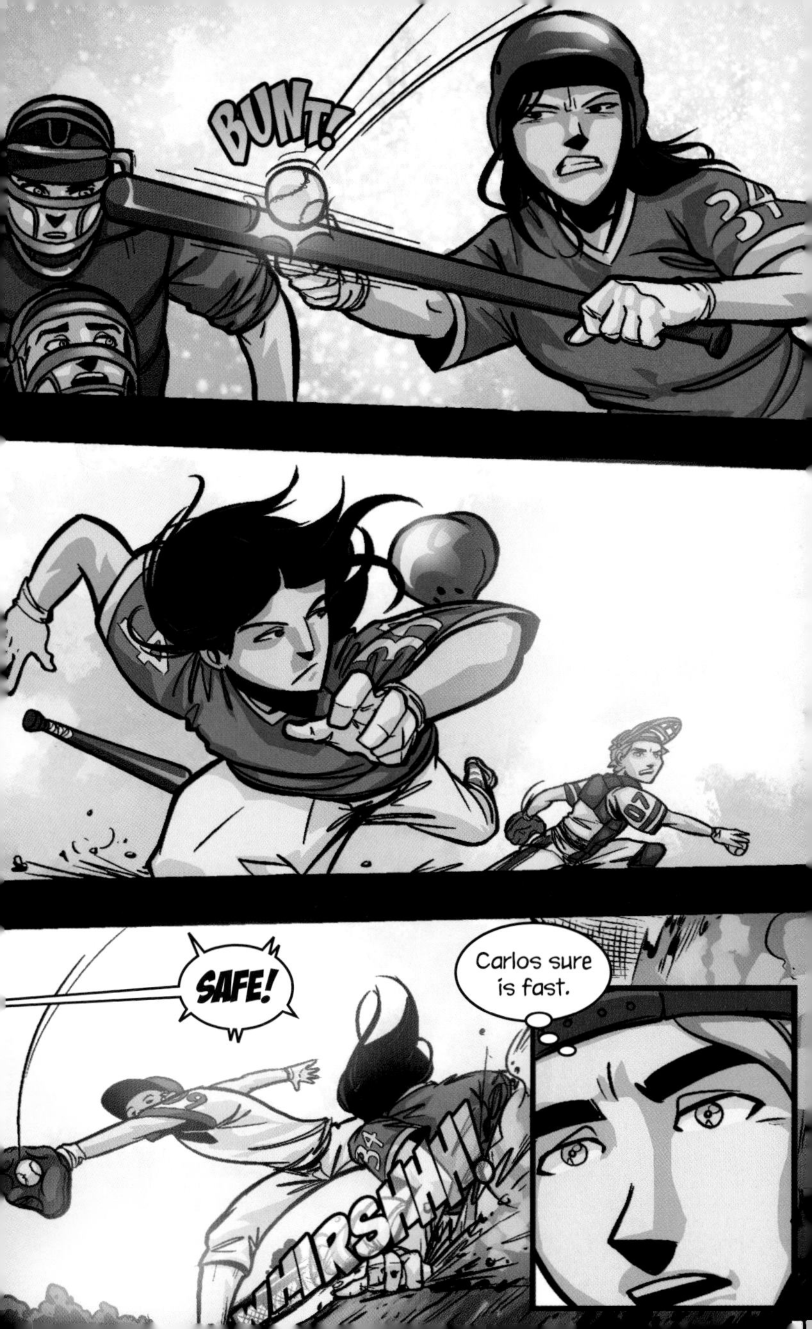
BUNT!
SAFE!
Carlos sure is fast.
WHIRSHHH!

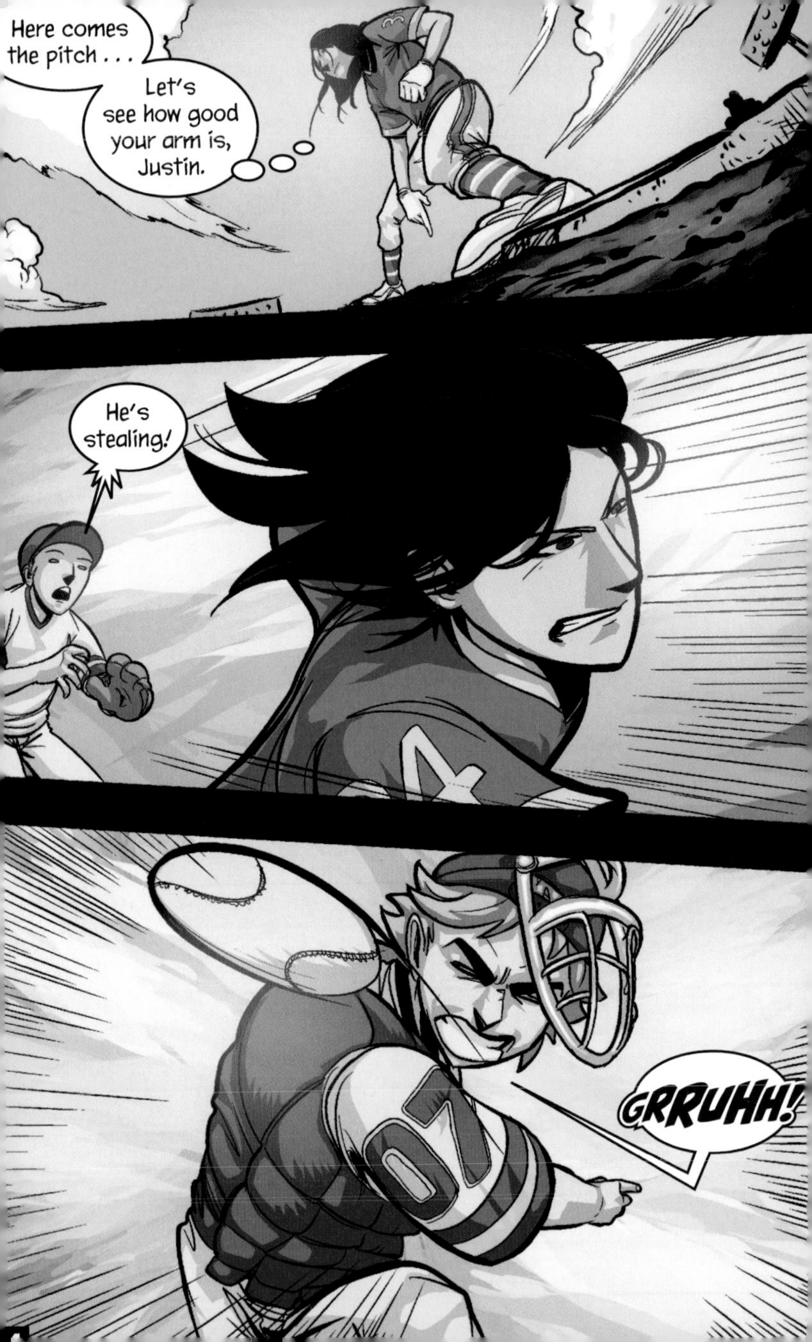
Here comes the pitch . . .
Let's see how good your arm is, Justin.
He's stealing!
GRRUHH!

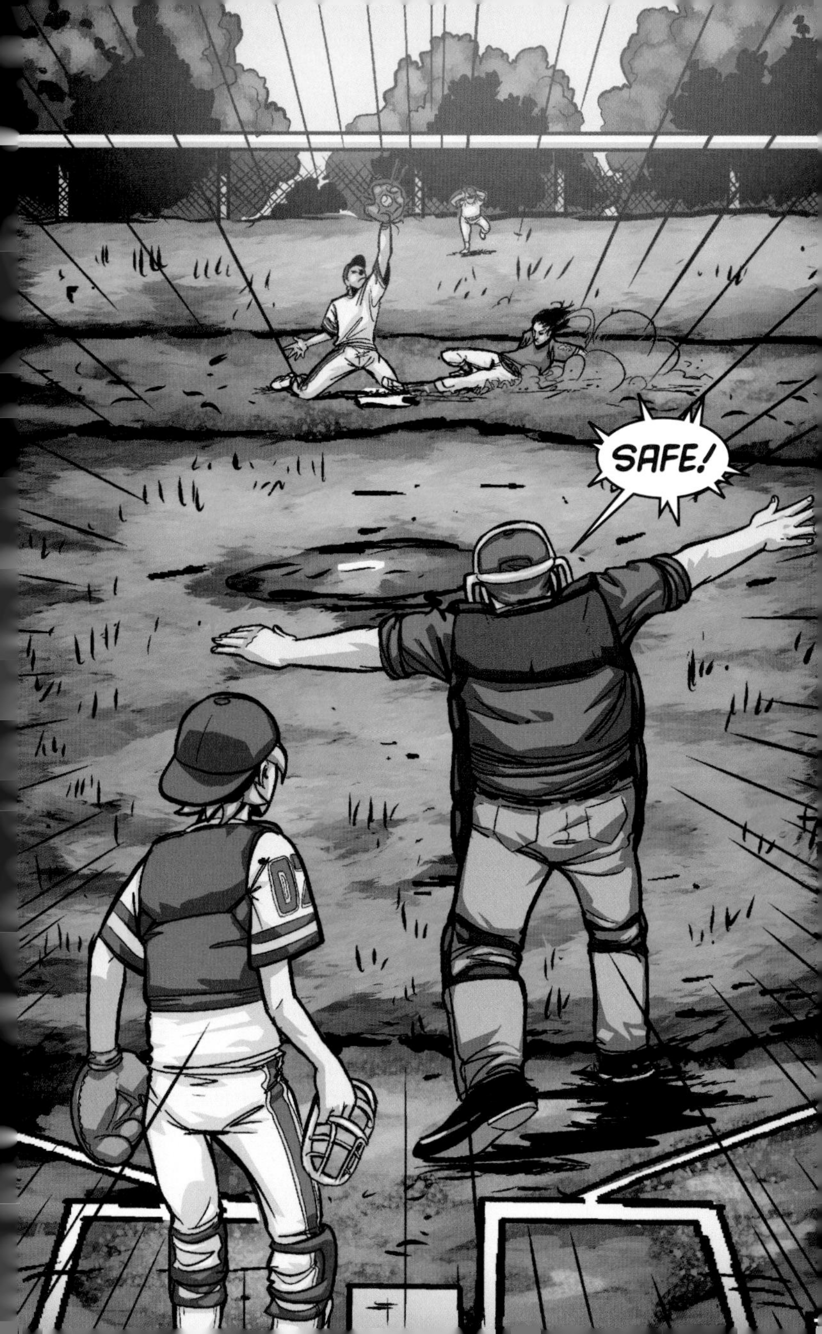
SAFE!

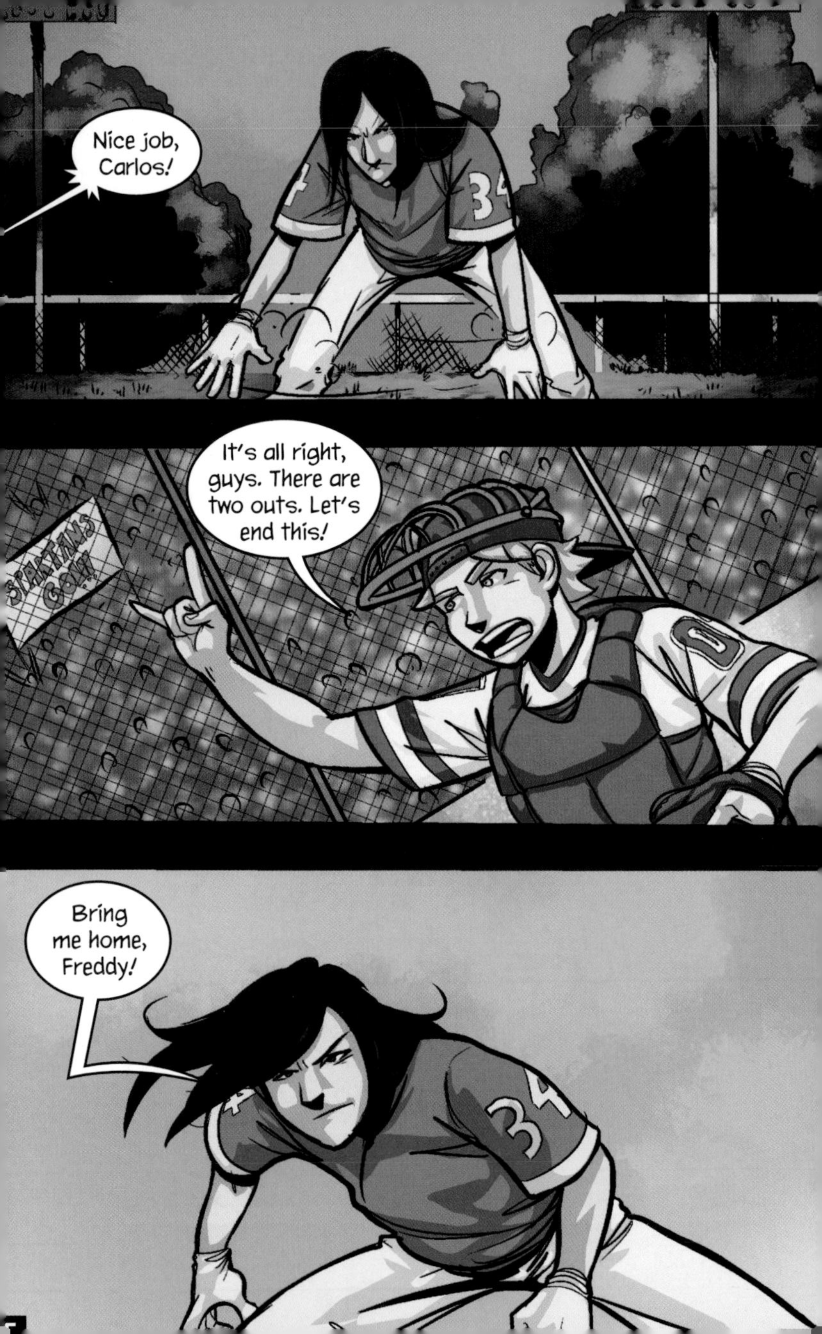
Nice job, Carlos!
It's all right, guys. There are two outs. Let's end this!
SPARTANS GO!!
Bring me home, Freddy!

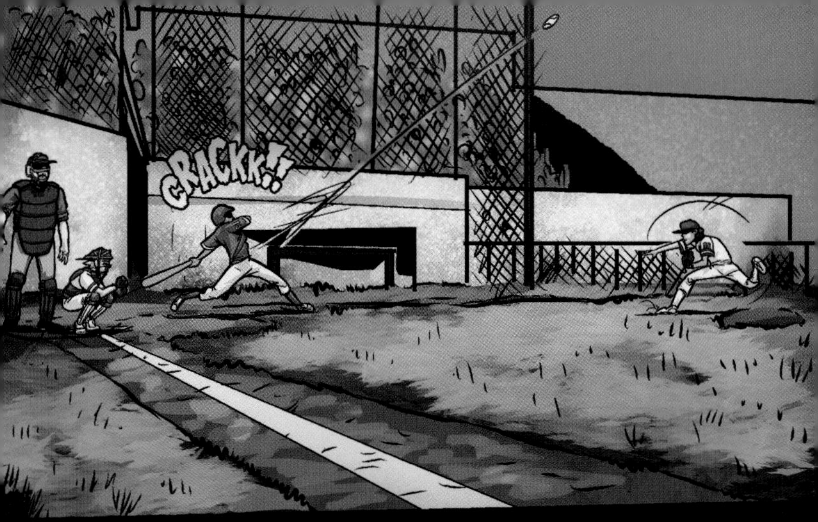
CRACKK!!

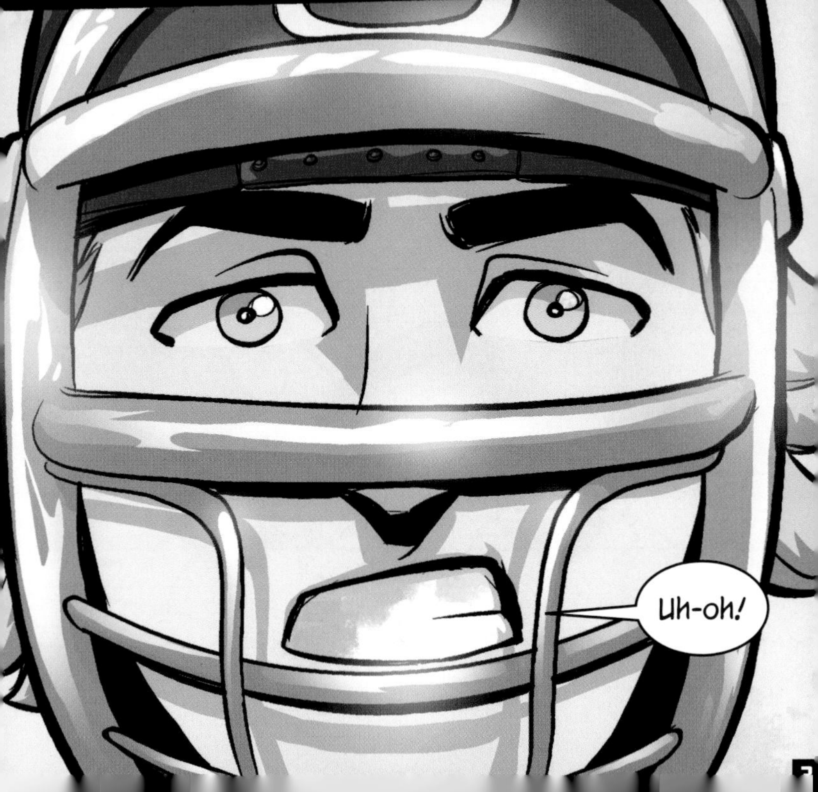
Uh-oh!

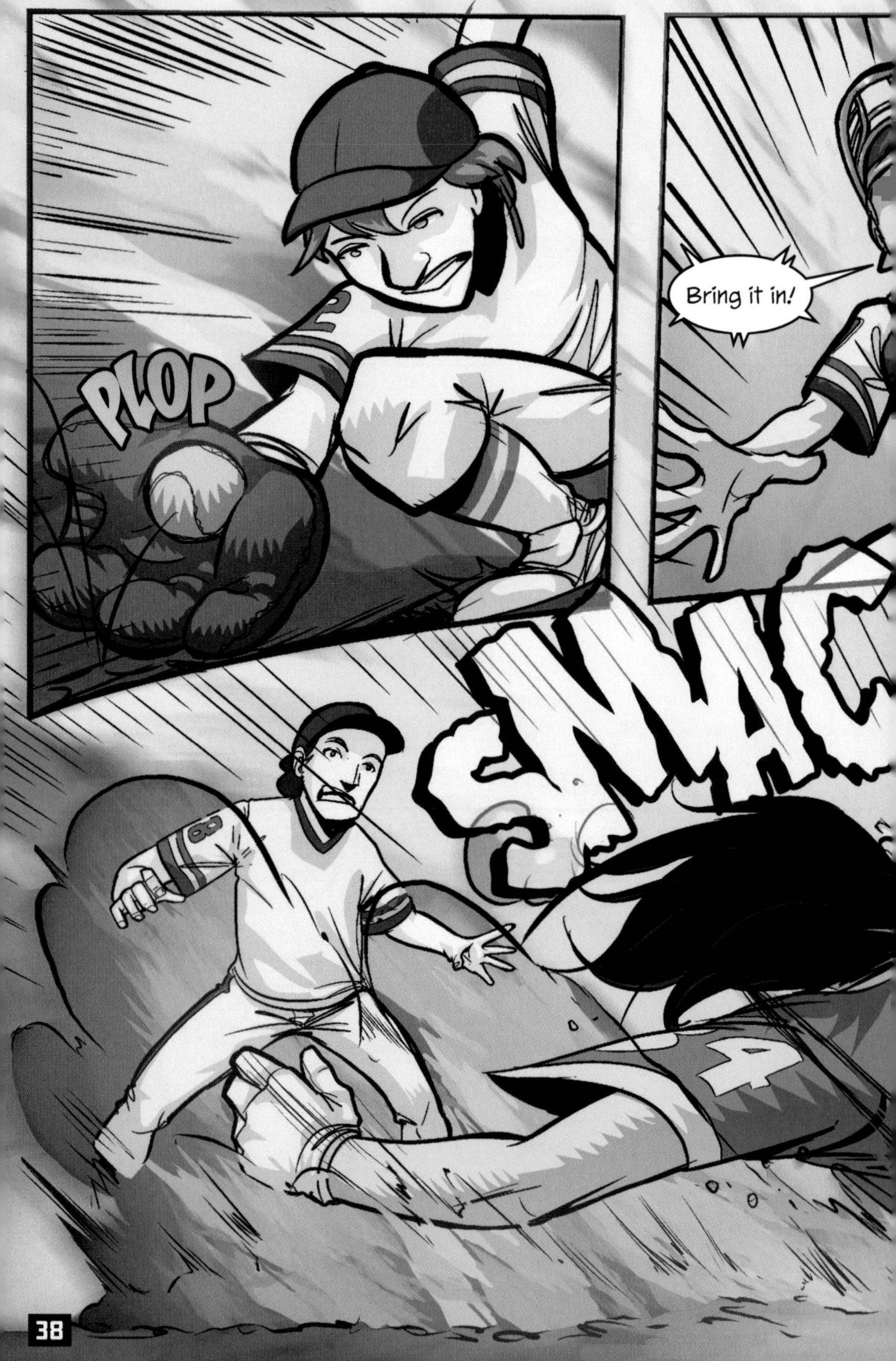
PLOP
Bring it in!
SMAC

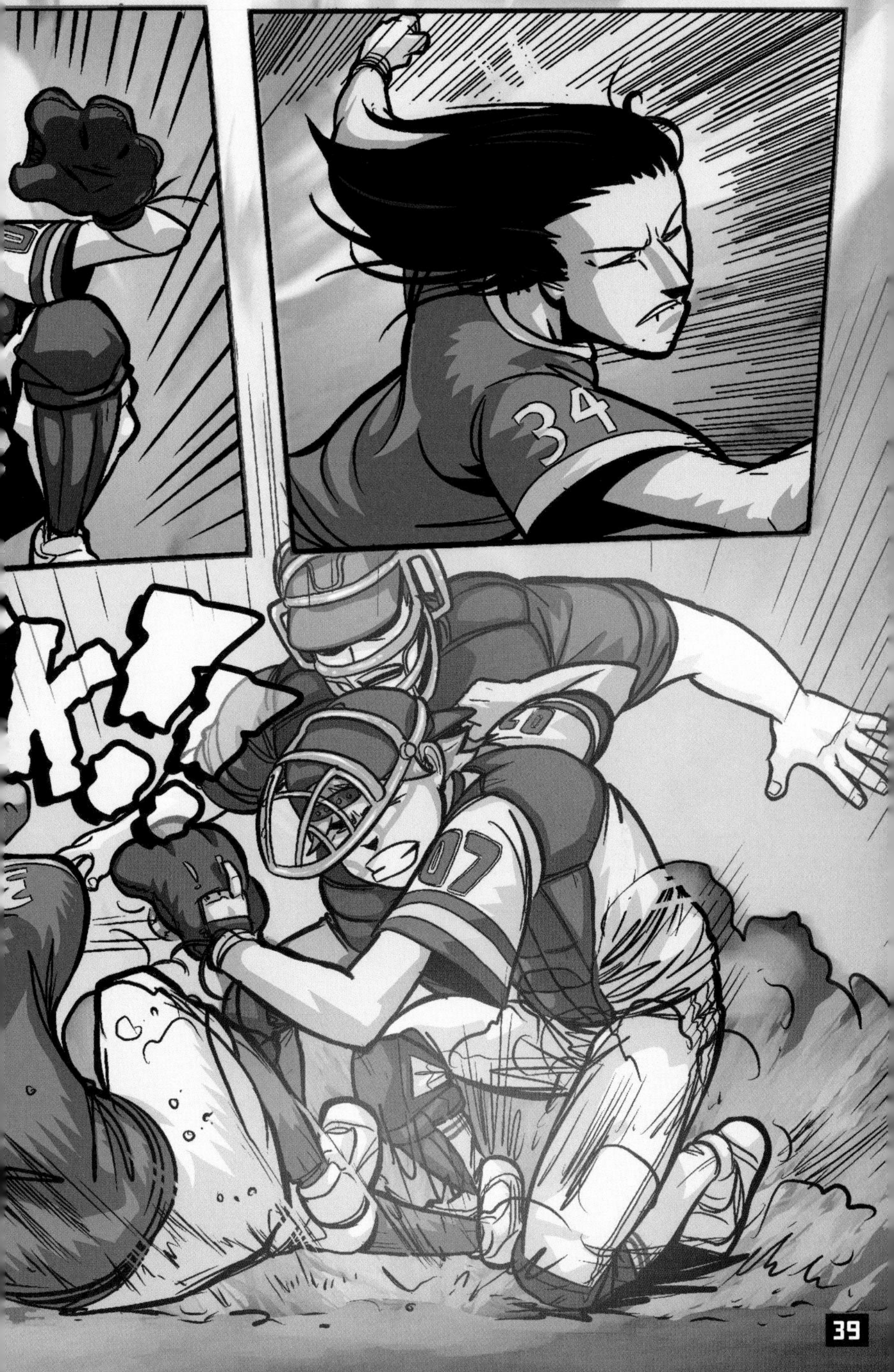
34
07

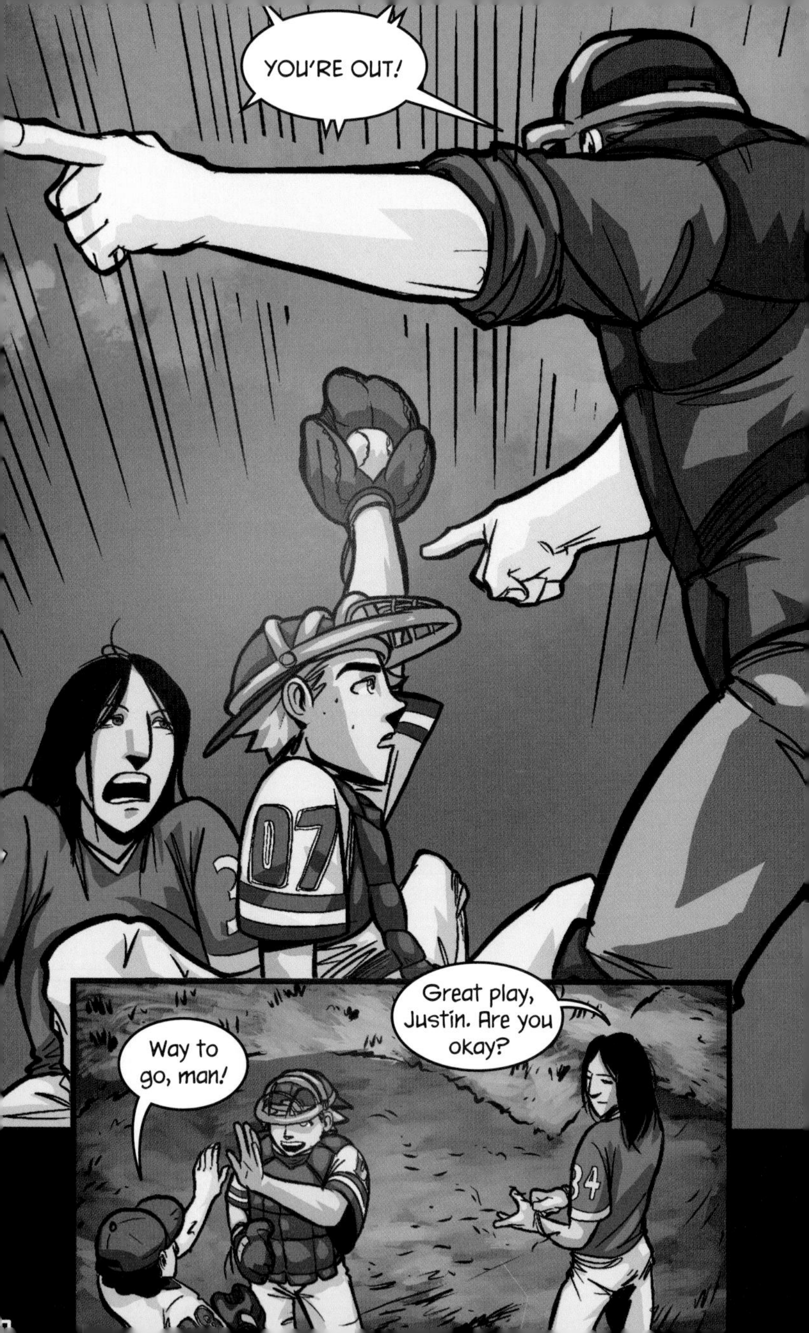
YOU'RE OUT!
Way to go, man!
Great play, Justin. Are you okay?

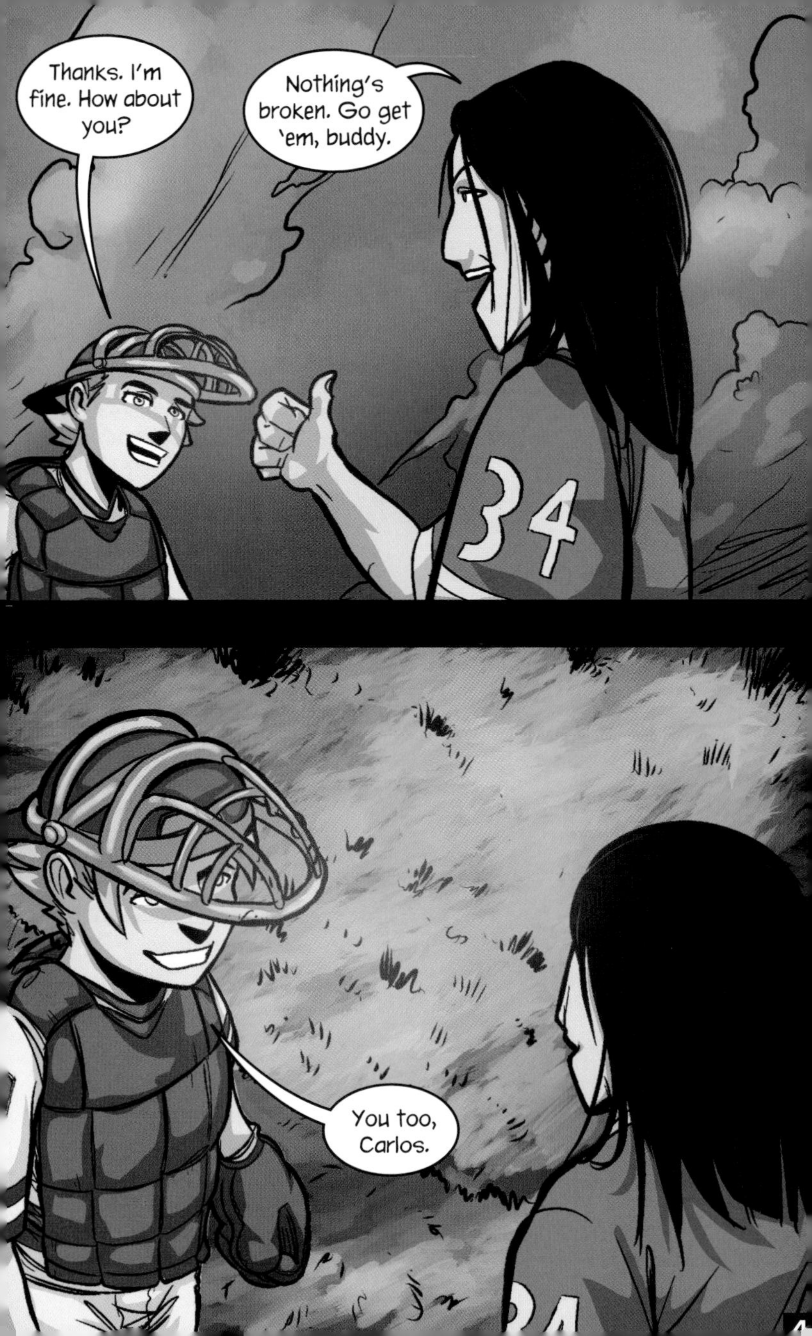
Thanks. I'm fine. How about you?
Nothing's broken. Go get 'em, buddy.
34
You too, Carlos.

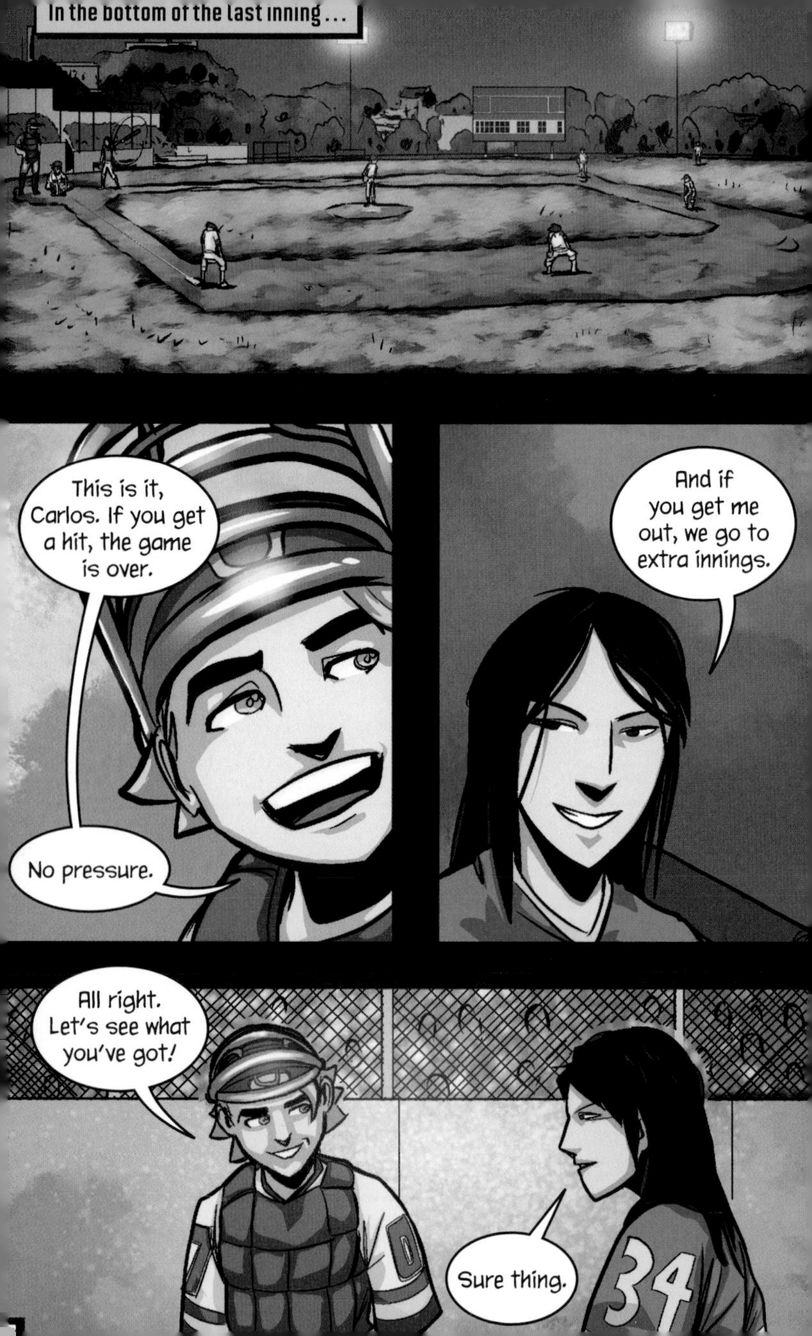
In the bottom of the last inning . . .
This is it, Carlos. If you get a hit, the game is over.
No pressure.
And if you get me out, we go to extra innings.
All right. Let's see what you've got!
Sure thing.
34

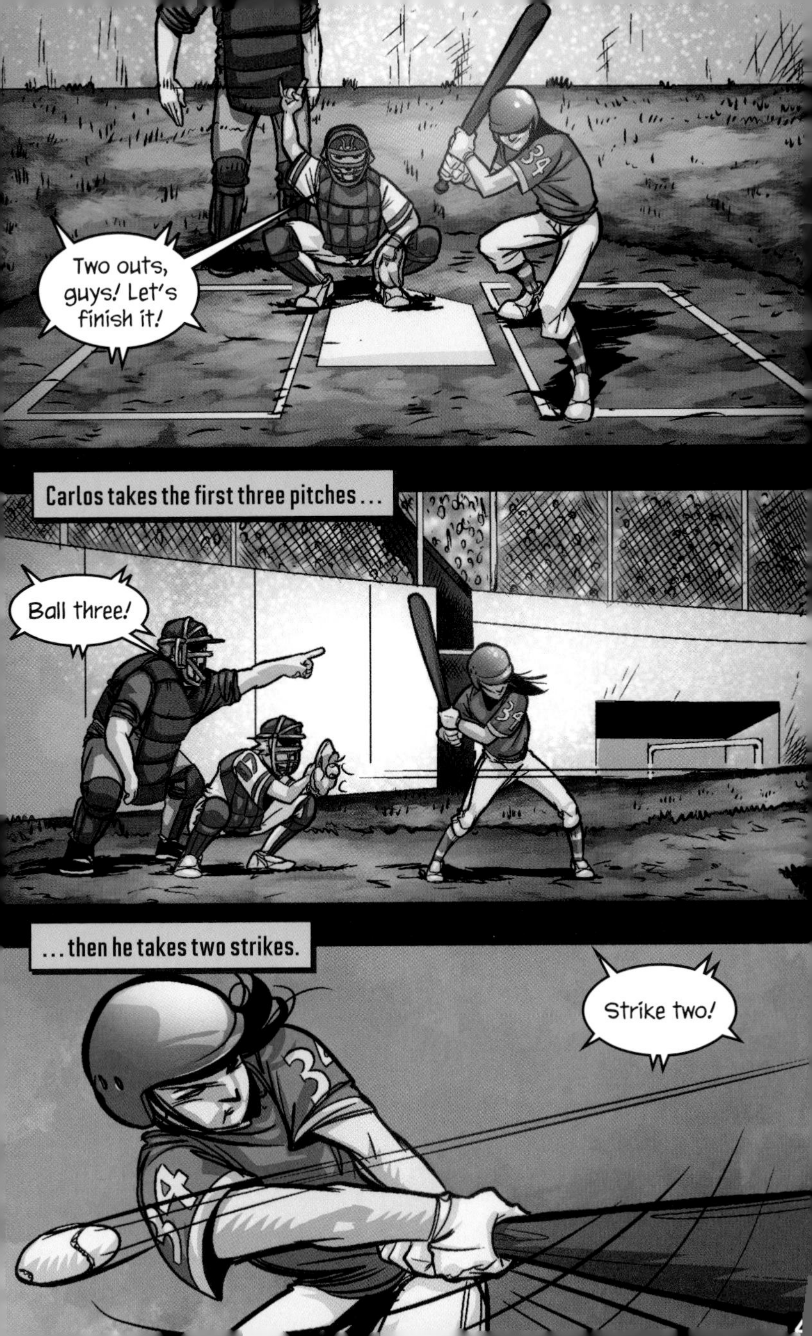
Two outs, guys! Let's finish it!
Carlos takes the first three pitches . . .
Ball three!
. . . then he takes two strikes.
Strike two!

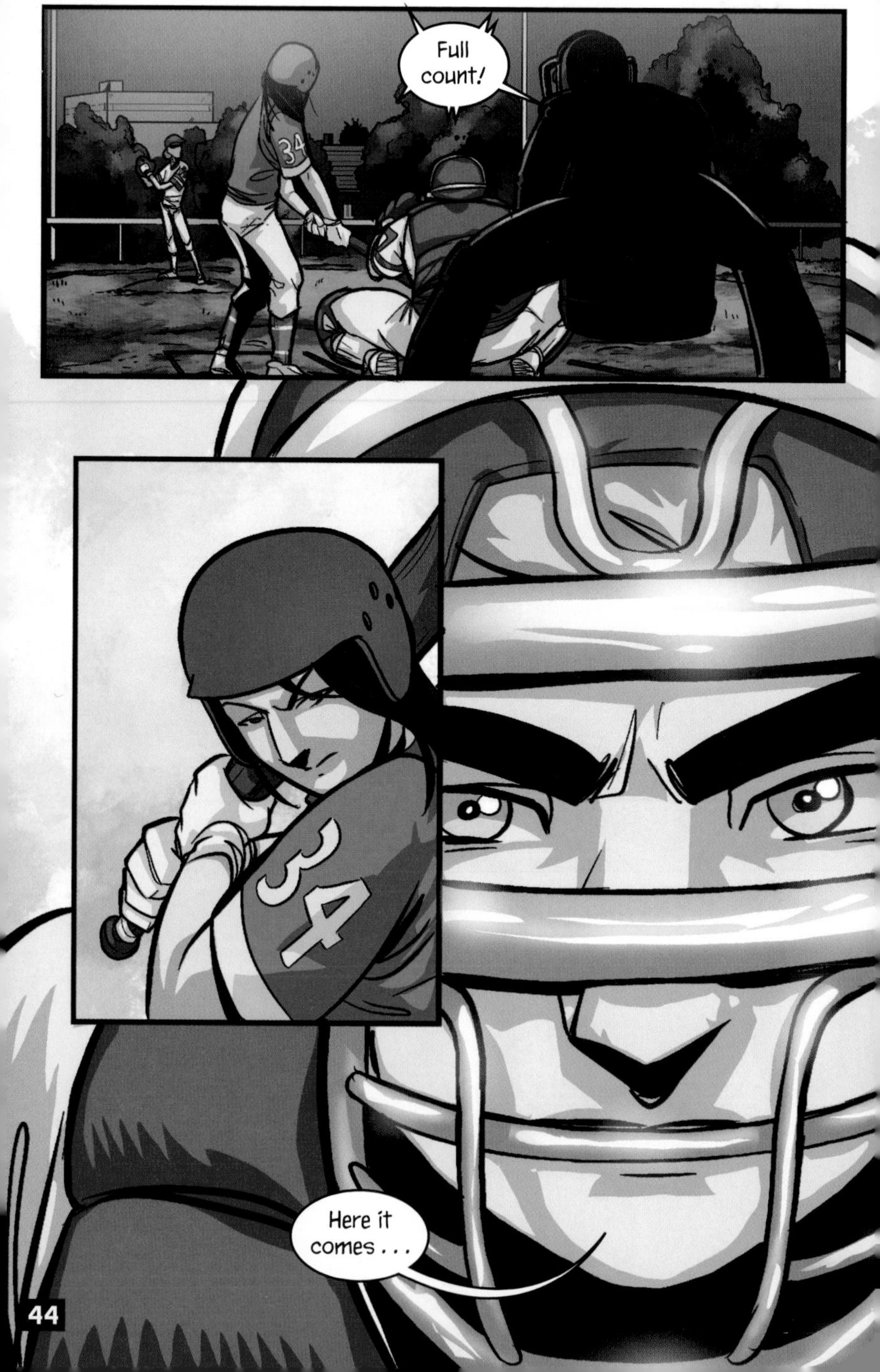
Full count!
Here it comes . . .

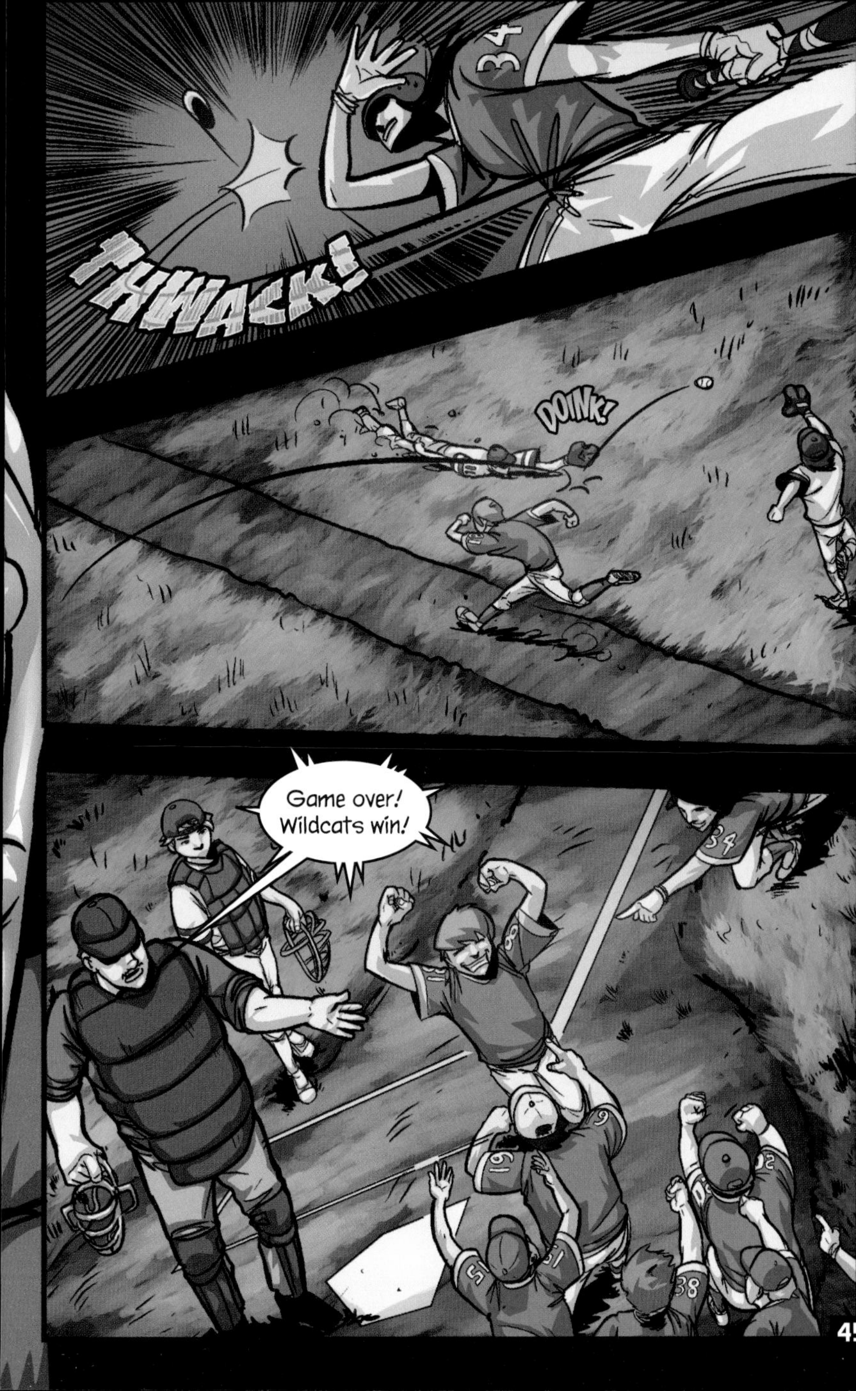
THWACK!
DOINK!
Game over! Wildcats win!

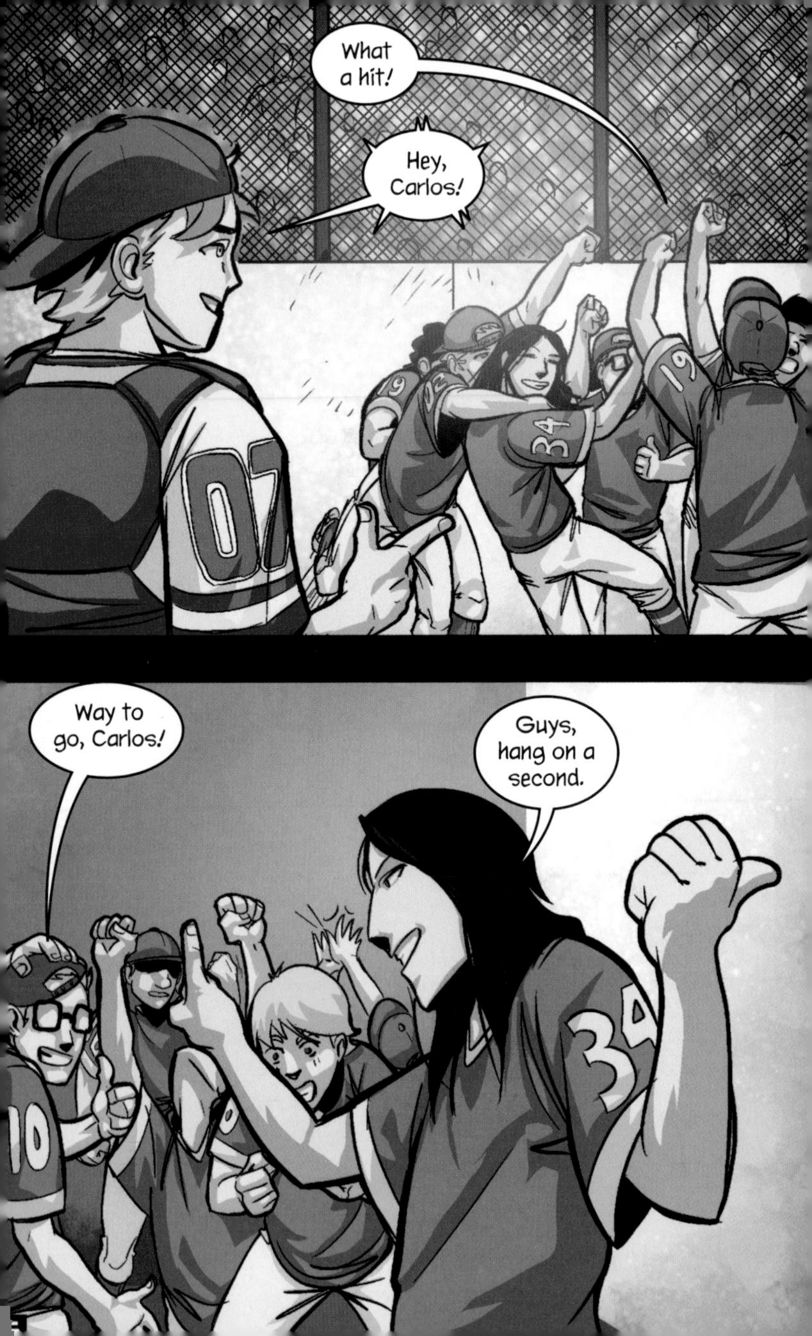
What a hit!
Hey, Carlos!
Way to go, Carlos!
Guys, hang on a second.

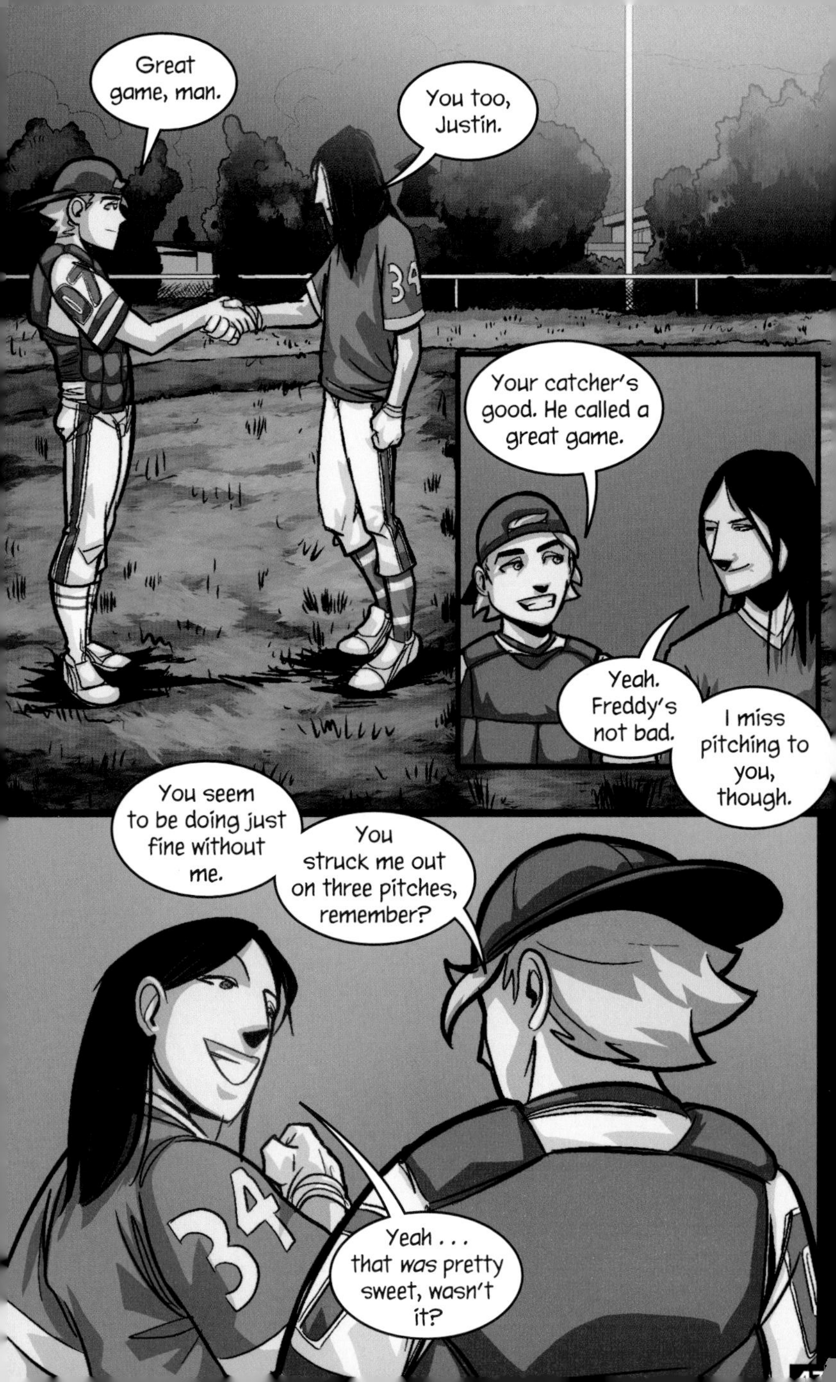

Great game, man.
You too, Justin.
Your catcher's good. He called a great game.
Yeah. Freddy's not bad.
I miss pitching to you, though.
You seem to be doing just fine without me.
You struck me out on three pitches, remember?
Yeah . . . that was pretty sweet, wasn't it?

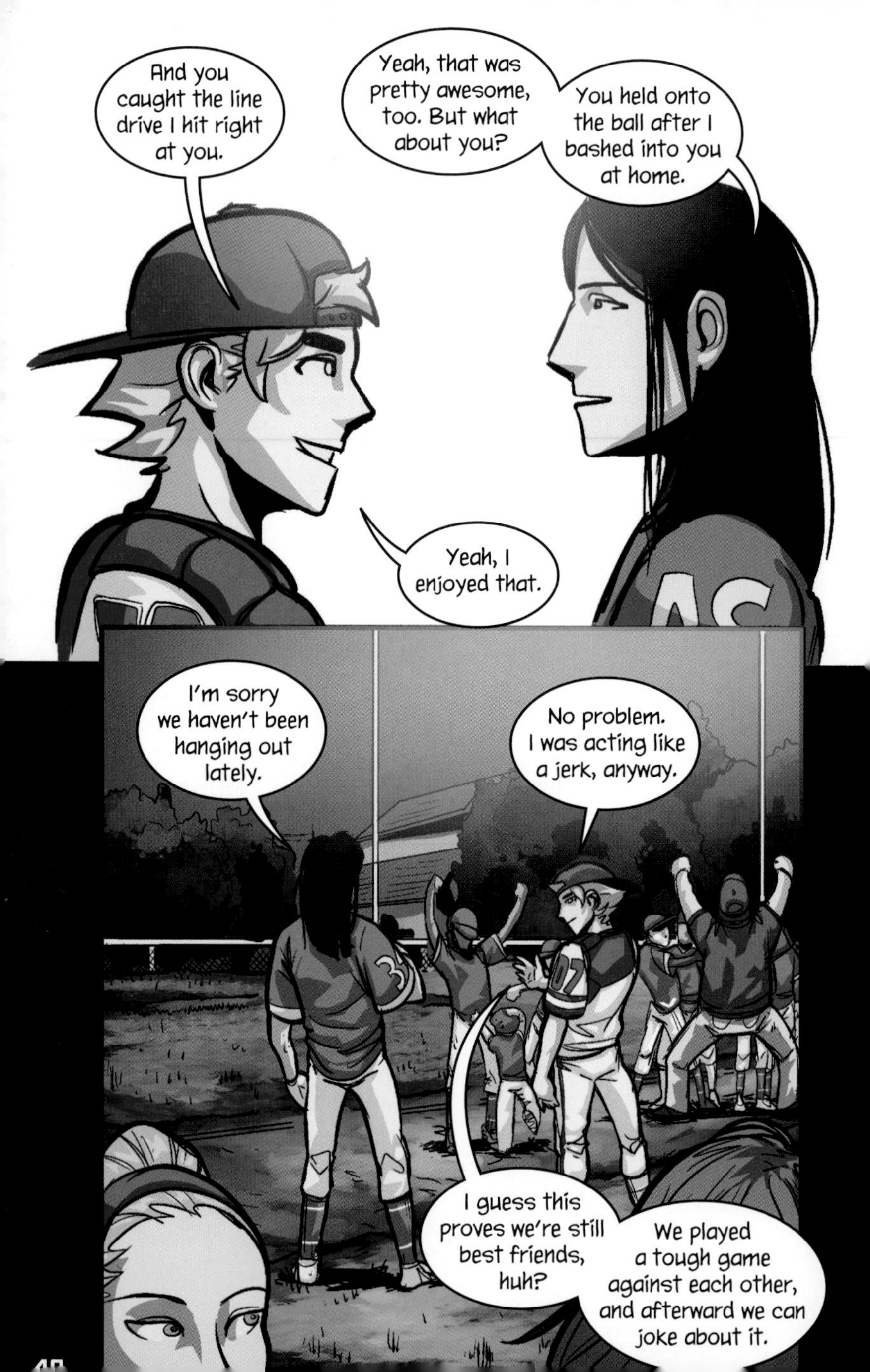
And you caught the line drive I hit right at you.
Yeah, that was pretty awesome, too. But what about you?
You held onto the ball after I bashed into you at home.
Yeah, I enjoyed that.
I'm sorry we haven't been hanging out lately.
No problem. I was acting like a jerk, anyway.
I guess this proves we're still best friends, huh?
We played a tough game against each other, and afterward we can joke about it.

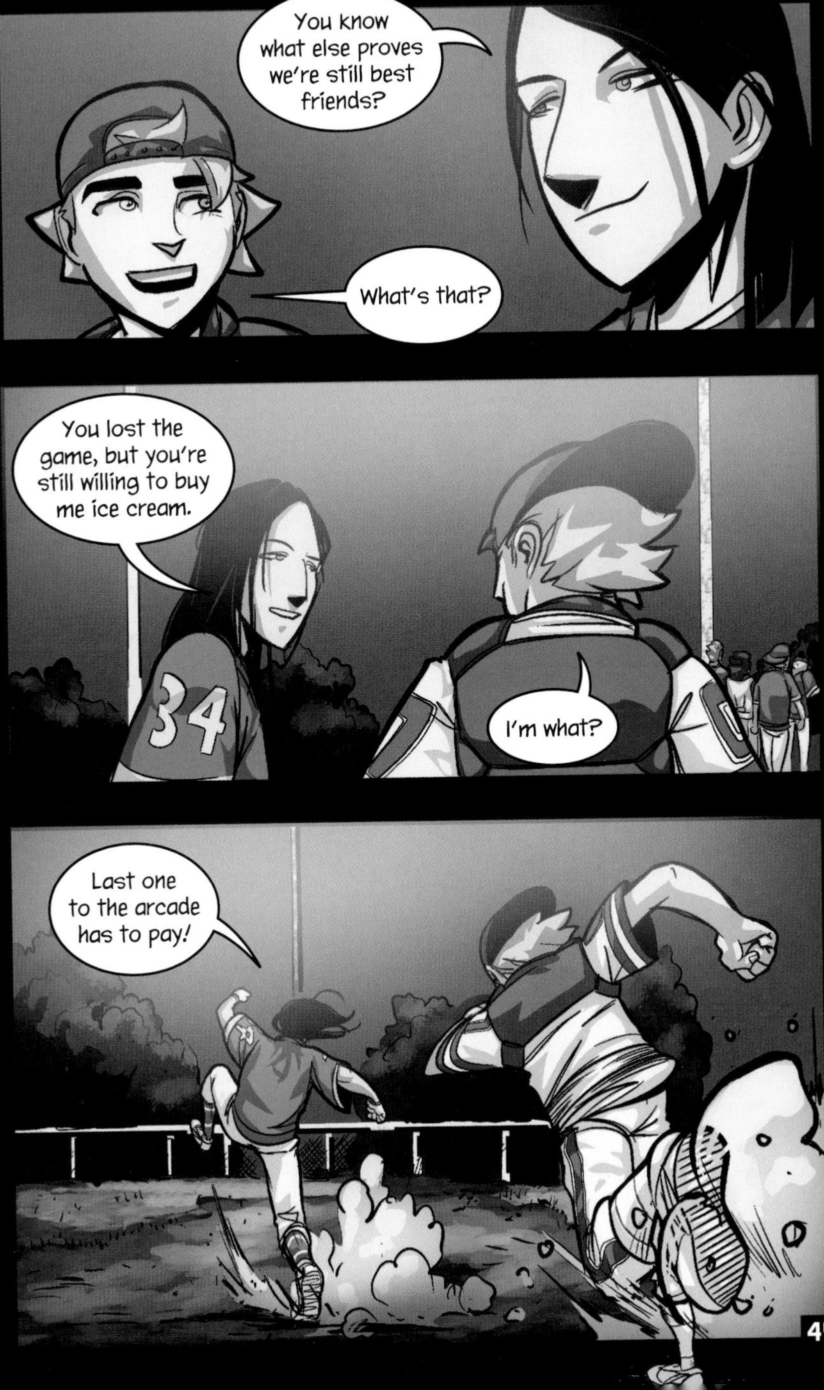
You know what else proves we're still best friends?
What's that?
You lost the game, but you're still willing to buy me ice cream.
I'm what?
Last one to the arcade has to pay!

SPORTS ZONE

STGAME RECAP

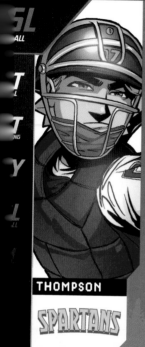

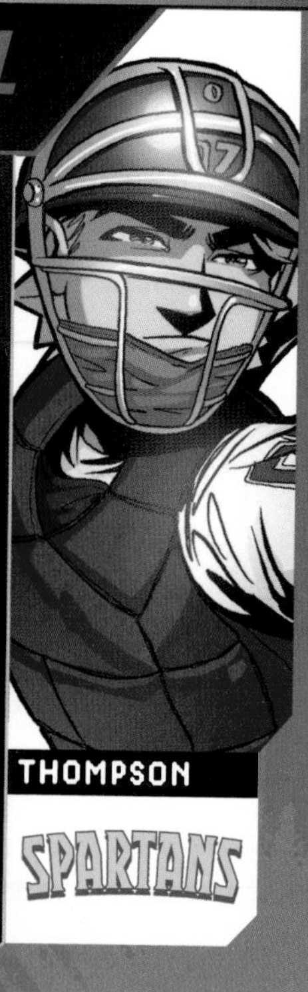
THOMPSON
SPARTANS

THE WILDCATS DEFEAT THE SPARTANS IN AN EPIC BASEBALL BATTLE!

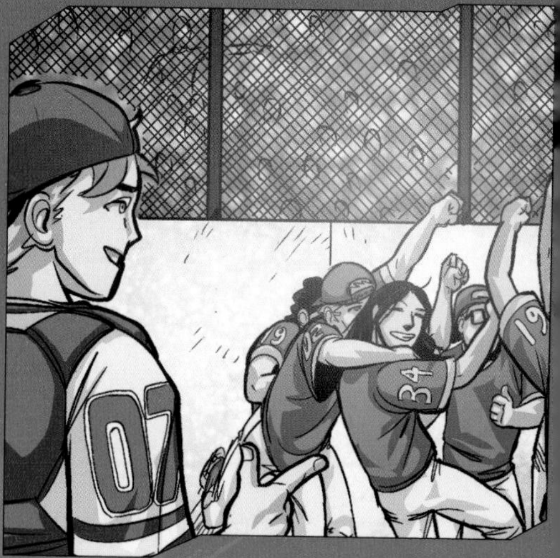

BY THE NUMBERS

GAME HIGHS:
HITS: LINCOLN, 3
RUNS: HERNANDEZ, 2
WALKS: THOMPSON, 2
STEALS: HERNANDEZ, 3
ERRORS: LENTZ, 2

STORY:
Fueled by the red-hot bat and searing pitches of Carlos Hernandez, the Wildcats edged out Justin's Spartans in a heated contest between friends. At one point during the game, the two best buds collided at home plate — but when the smoke cleared, both teens were unhurt, and grinning from ear to ear.

Sports Illustrated KIDS

UP NEXT: SI KIDS INFO CENTER

BLZ vs BKS 3-1
TGR vs RDR 33-32
EAG vs BAN 14-7
SPA vs WLD 4-3
BAN vs RDR 21-15
RZR vs LIG 4-3
BLZ vs BKS 3-1

SZ POSTGAME EXTRA

WHERE *YOU* ANALYZE THE GAME!

Baseball fans erupted in excitement when Carlos Hernandez and the Wildcats overcame Justin Thompson's Spartans by a single run. Let's go into the stands and ask some fans for their perspectives on today's game . . .

DISCUSSION QUESTION 1

Best friends Justin and Carlos were forced to compete against each other. Can opponents be friends, or should they be enemies?

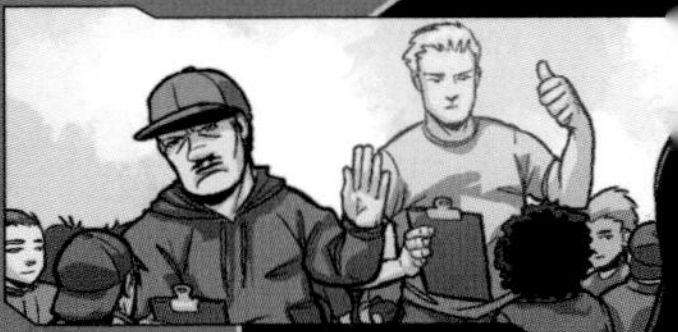

DISCUSSION QUESTION 2

Carlos and Justin struggled to save their friendship. Who was more to blame for the tension between the two best friends — Carlos or Justin? Why?

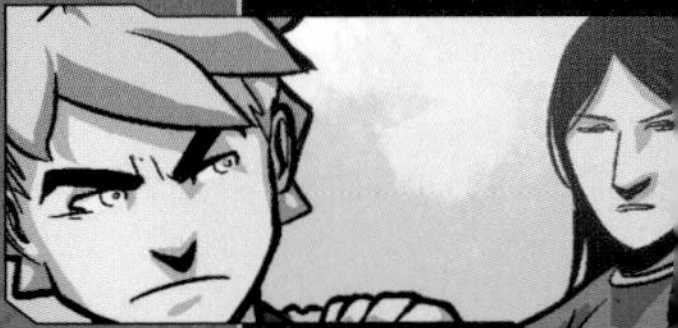

WRITING PROMPT 1

The Spartans and Wildcats end up playing each other again in the playoffs. Who will win? How will the two friends act? Write the next part of this story.

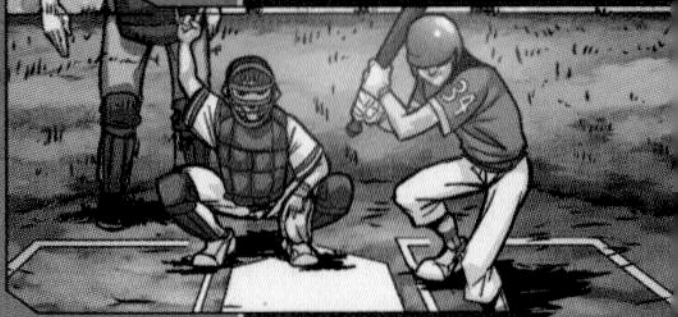

WRITING PROMPT 2

Have you ever had to compete against a close friend in a contest of some kind? Write about it.

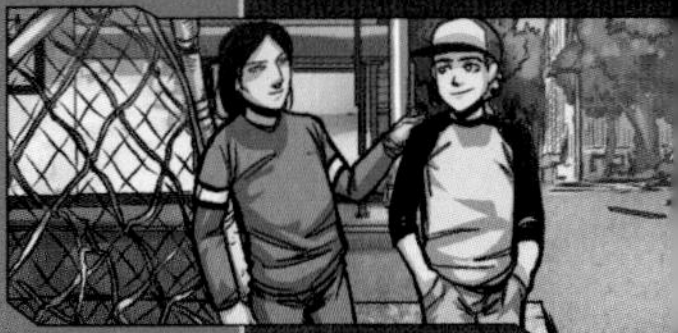

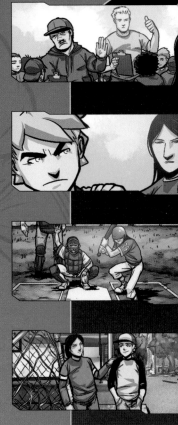

(ar-KADE)—an area containing a variety of video games that can be played for a fee

(DUH-buhl PLAY)—a defensive play that results in two base runners being called out

(EP-ik)—if something is epic, it is either heroic, impressive, or very important

(EK-struh IN-ingz)—if a game is tied when the bottom of the ninth inning is over, then the game continues until a winner is determined

(LINE DRIVE)—a ball that is hit into the air at a low angle going so fast that it travels in a straight line through the field

(ON DEK)—a phrase that refers to the next batter up in the inning. This person stands in a designated circle next to the batter's box and warms up before batting.

EATORS

CHRIS KREIE › Author

Chris Kreie lives in Minnesota with his wife and two children. He works as a school librarian, and writes children's books in his free time.

JESUS ABURTO › Illustrator

Jesus Aburto was born in Monterrey, Mexico. He has been a graphic designer, a colorist, and an illustrator. Aburto has colored popular comic book characters, such as Wolverine, Blade, and Nightwing. In 2008, Aburto joined Protobunker Studio, where he enjoys working as a full-time comic book illustrator.

FARES MAESE › Colorist

Fares Maese is an illustrator and graphic designer born in Monterrey, Mexico. Fares has worked with Marvel, Fantasy Flight Games, and Paizo Publishing, and is currently partnering with Ponxlab Studio, where he enjoys working as an illustrator and colorist.

ANDRES ESPARZA › Colorist

Andres Esparza was born in Monterrey, Mexico. In the 1980s, Andres's brother got him hooked on comic books. Since then, Andres has created logos, illustrations, and character designs for several different companies. Andres contributes to a local comic book called *Melanie*, and an alternative magazine called *PONX*.

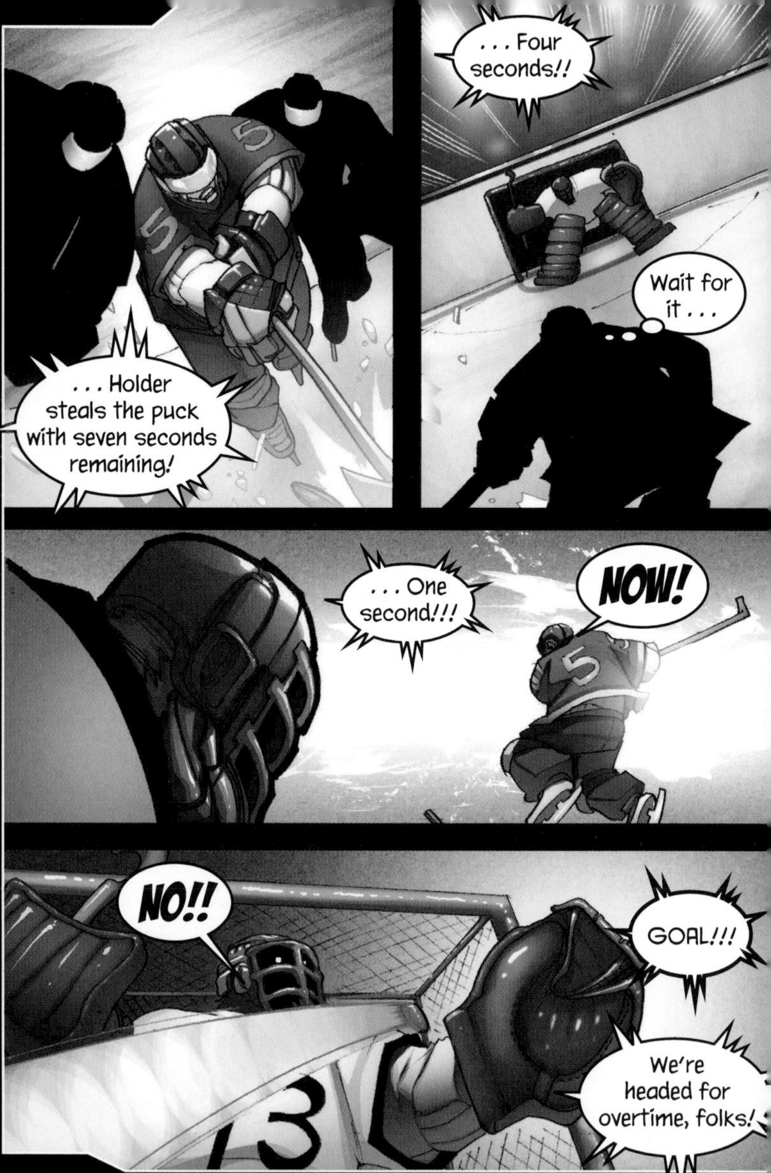
. . . Holder steals the puck with seven seconds remaining!
. . . Four seconds!!
Wait for it . . .
. . . One second!!!
NOW!
NO!!
GOAL!!!
We're headed for overtime, folks!

HOT SPORTS. HOT FORMAT!

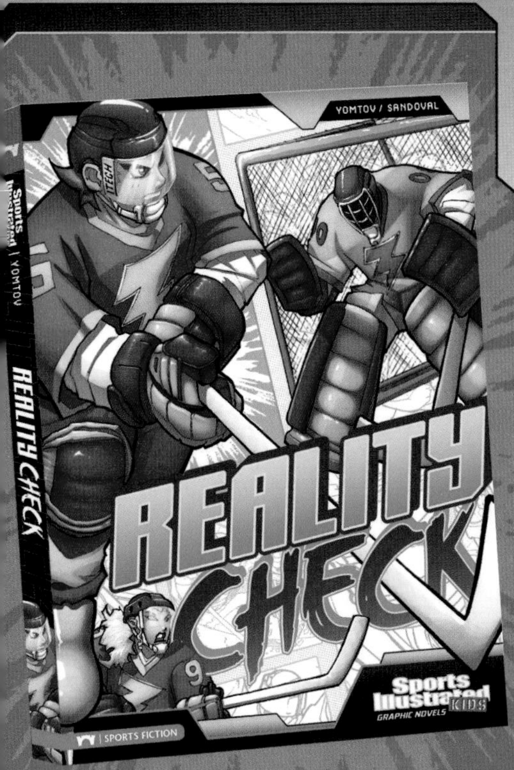
YOMTOV / SANDOVAL
REALITY CHECK
Sports Illustrated KIDS
GRAPHIC NOVELS
SPORTS FICTION
Sports Illustrated | YOMTOV
REALITY CHECK

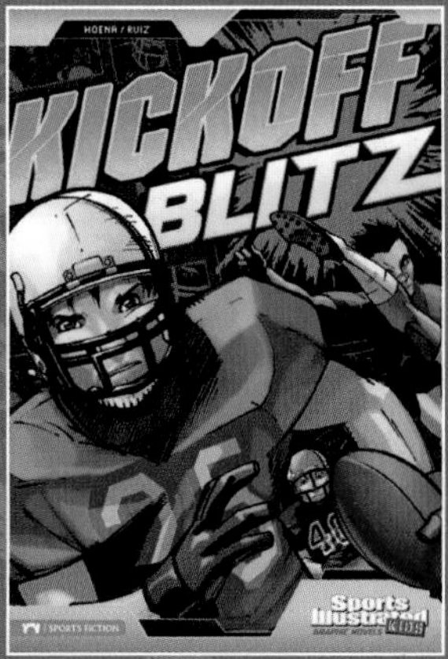
HOENA / RUIZ
KICKOFF BLITZ
SPORTS FICTION
Sports Illustrated KIDS
GRAPHIC NOVELS

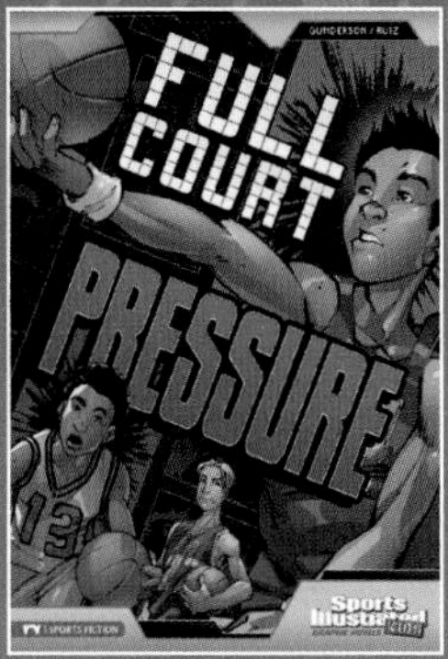
GUNDERSON / RUIZ
FULL COURT PRESSURE
SPORTS FICTION
Sports Illustrated KIDS
GRAPHIC NOVELS

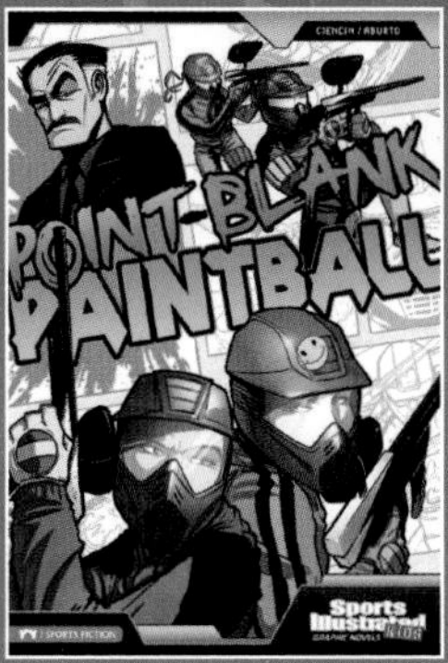
CIENCIN / ABURTO
POINT-BLANK PAINTBALL
SPORTS FICTION
Sports Illustrated KIDS
GRAPHIC NOVELS

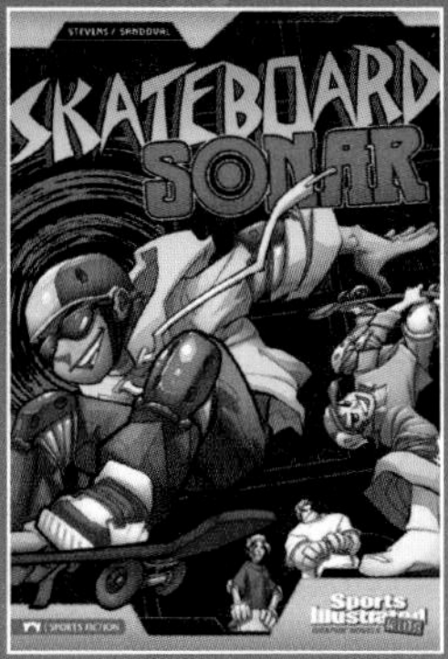
STEVENS / SANDOVAL
SKATEBOARD SONAR
SPORTS FICTION
Sports Illustrated KIDS
GRAPHIC NOVELS

GREAT CHARACTERS BATTLE FOR SPORTS GLORY IN TODAY'S HOTTEST FORMAT—GRAPHIC NOVELS!

ONLY FROM STONE ARCH BOOKS

Sports Illustrated KIDS GRAPHIC NOVELS

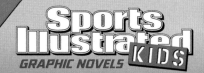

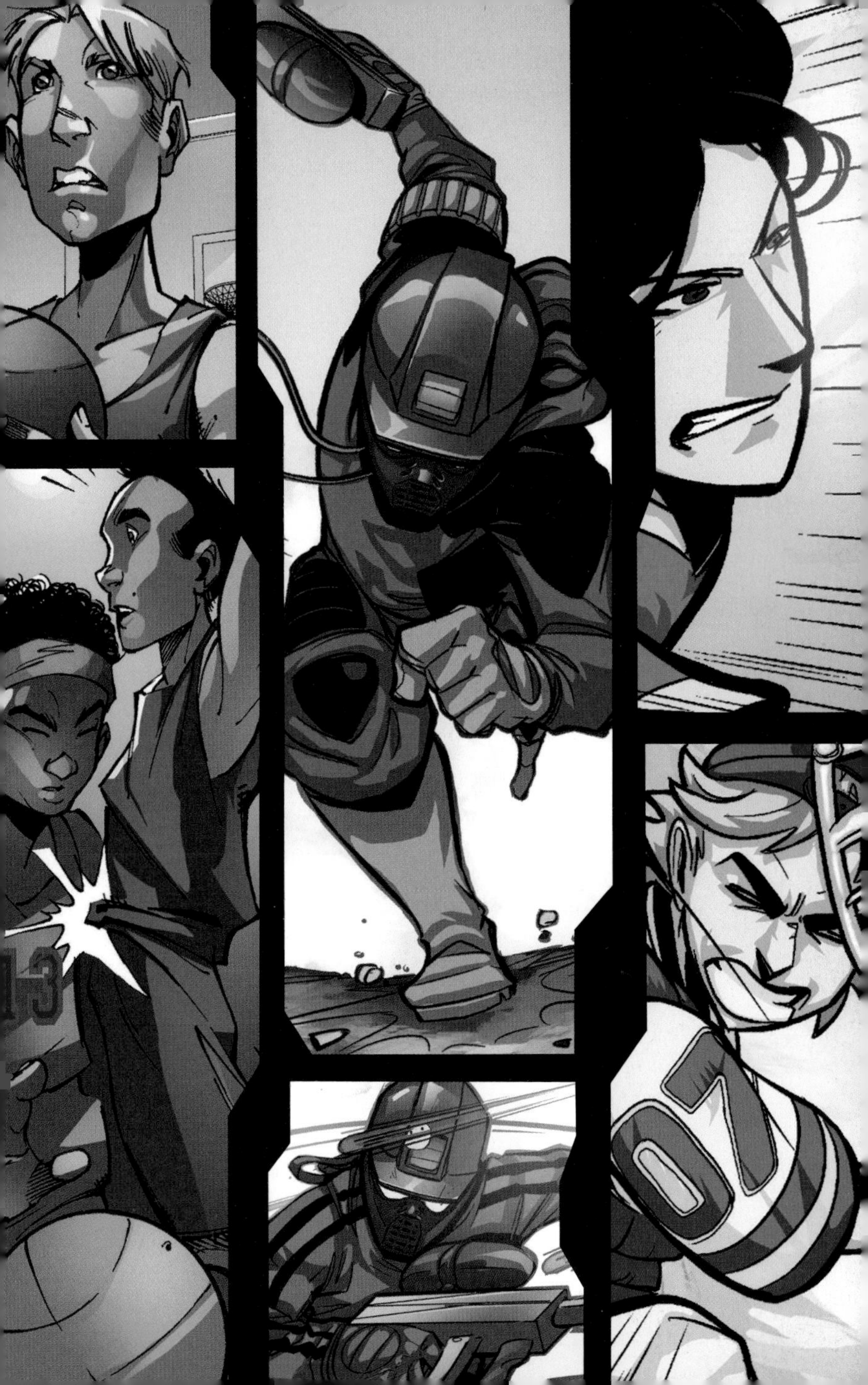

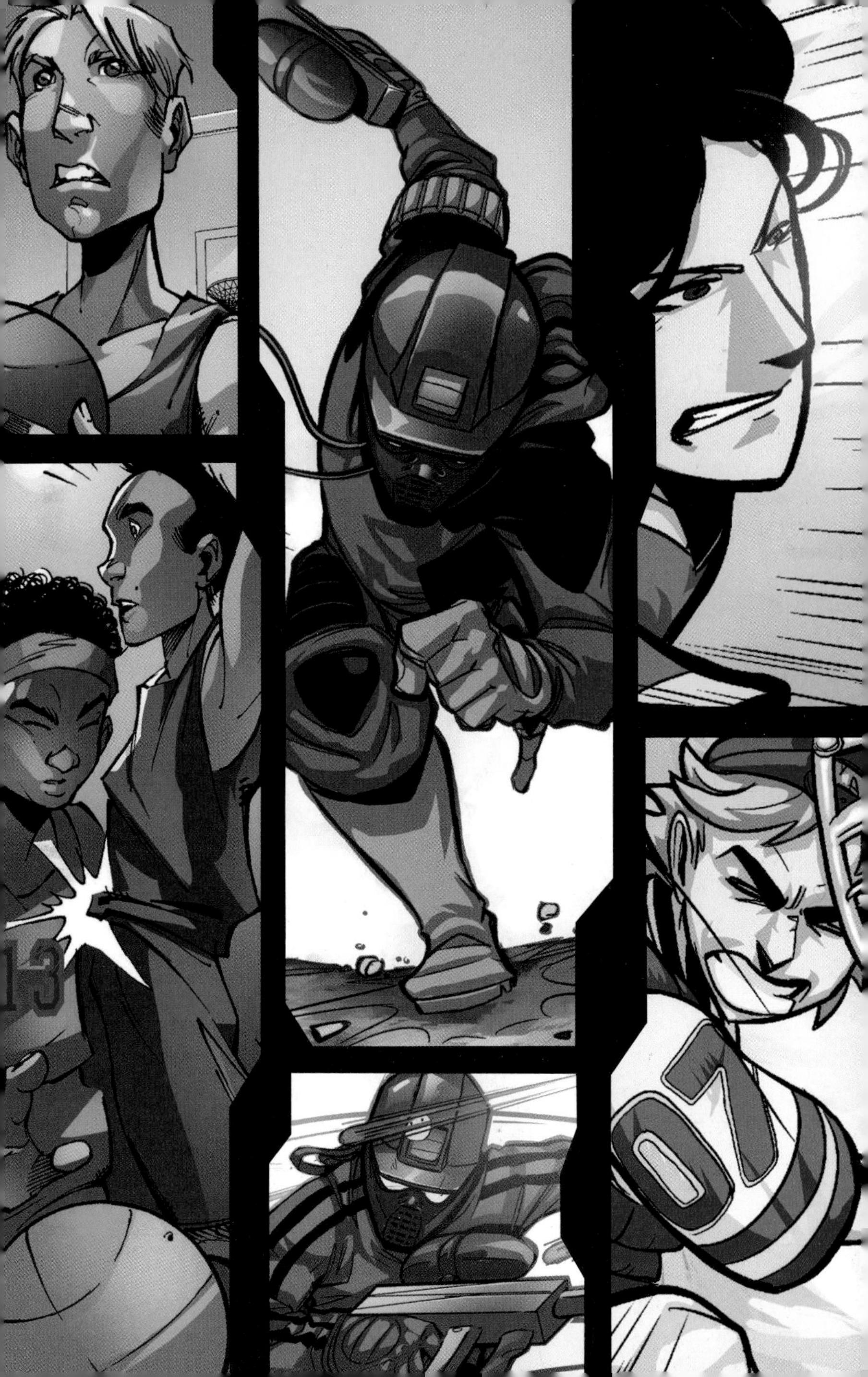

Sports Illustrated KIDS

GRAPHIC NOVELS

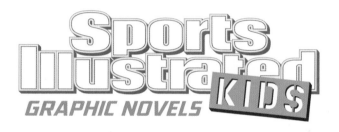

STONE ARCH BOOKS
a capstone imprint